GIRL FIVE:

BOUND

(A Maya Gray FBI Suspense Thriller—Book 5)

Molly Black

Molly Black

Bestselling author Molly Black is author of the MAYA GRAY FBI suspense thriller series, comprising nine books (and counting); the RYLIE WOLF FBI suspense thriller series, comprising six books (and counting); of the TAYLOR SAGE FBI suspense thriller series, comprising three books (and counting); and of the KATIE WINTER FBI suspense thriller series, comprising six books (and counting).

An avid reader and lifelong fan of the mystery and thriller genres, Molly loves to hear from you, so please feel free to visit www.mollyblackauthor.com to learn more and stay in touch.

ISBN: 978-1-0943-9450-3

"Why are we talking about Juliet's love life?" Clarissa demanded. "*I'm* the one who just got engaged."

She got to both play the Good Samaritan saving Juliet and bring the attention back to herself. This was *her* night.

"Does Hank know what he's getting into?" Mary asked.

"He'd better know by now," Clarissa replied. "Besides, it's just the right time to do it."

"Oh, you're ready to settle down, are you?" Sandy asked, with a snort, as if the thought of Clarissa doing *that* were simply impossible to imagine.

"Maybe," Clarissa said in a defensive tone. "I could settle down if I *wanted* to."

The others laughed at that.

"But do you want to?" Juliet asked.

"Hell no," Clarissa said, and waved at one of the waiters in the bar. "Another round here!"

He came over with the drinks, giving Clarissa an appreciative smile as he did so. Plenty of other guys in the room were looking her way too. Well, *maybe* some of them were looking at her friends, but Clarissa wanted to believe that it was mostly her.

"I bet you could take home any guy in the room right now," Mary said. She probably meant it as a compliment, but Clarissa guessed that she was also trying to cause trouble.

"I'm about to be a married woman!" Clarissa pointed out.

She saw Sandy give a one-shouldered shrug. "So enjoy your last nights of freedom."

It was tempting, obviously. There were plenty of hot guys there, and it wasn't as if Clarissa intended to be *completely* tied down, just because she was marrying Hank. Even though she really did love him, and genuinely wanted to spend her life with him. At the same time, though, she knew that if she did anything in front of Mary, pictures, and probably video, would make it back to Hank before Clarissa could even start to get her excuses in order.

"And will any of *those* guys buy me a ring like this?" Clarissa replied, flashing her engagement ring for probably the hundredth time that night. Diamonds sparkled the same blue as her eyes, glittering under the lights of the bar, catching the glare of small spotlights set around the room.

Her friends cooed over it. They knew expensive when they saw it. They might make fun of the idea of settling down, or being limited to just one man for the rest of their lives, but they knew what a ring like this cost. Clarissa knew as well as anyone that you couldn't put a price tag on love, but she was pretty sure that her friends had managed to put one on the ring.

"Shots?" Sandy suggested.

Clarissa shook her head. "I should get going. I have a meeting with a wedding planner in the morning."

"You're going to be *such* a bridezilla," Mary said.

"That's the plan," Clarissa replied, forcing a smile. She tried to imagine what kind of horrible bridesmaid's dress she could get Mary into for this. That thought lent a genuine edge to the smile. "Anyway, I've got to go."

"Are you sure?" Juliet asked.

"We're just starting to have fun," Sandy said.

Clarissa waved off their token efforts to get her to stay, heading for the front of the bar. She collected her coat and started out into the night, back toward where she'd left her car. She was pretty sure she was fine to drive. Probably.

She'd only parked a little way from the bar, out on the street, so Clarissa walked to her car, high heels clicking on the sidewalk as she hurried. She was almost there when she saw a man approaching, a hooded top pulled up so she couldn't see his features.

For a moment, Clarissa was puzzled. Was this some guy who'd seen her in the bar and wanted a last chance to try to hit on her? Then she saw the knife, and realized what this had to be: a mugging.

Clarissa held up her hands, the diamond ring catching the light of a street lamp.

"Look, whatever this is, I'll—"

The man didn't say anything, just stepped forward, grabbing her. His right hand pumped forward, and Clarissa felt the impact of it. It felt like she'd been punched in the chest, but she knew in that moment that she'd been stabbed.

The man drew his arm back and stabbed her again, then again.

Clarissa wanted to scream, but suddenly she didn't have any breath, she couldn't get any air. She felt her legs going weak, and collapsed to her knees. From there, she fell onto her back on the sidewalk, staring up at her attacker.

He still didn't say anything, or maybe Clarissa couldn't hear it. The whole world was closing in around her now as he knelt beside her. He just watched her, looking down at her as if he could see the life ebbing out of her.

Clarissa wanted to ask him why. She wanted to tell him that he had to let her live, because she was going to get married. She didn't have the strength for it, though. All she could do was lie there, staring up, while the blackness closed in and claimed her.

CHAPTER TWO

Maya looked around her new unit in a corner of the fourth floor, proud of the small group they had. Just a week or two ago, it had been only her, helped on an informal basis by Detective Marco Spinelli of the Cleveland PD.

Now he was there as an official part of the team, tall, lean, muscled frame hunched over a desk as he tried to run down connections between the Moonlight Killer's hostages, his "bunnies." He was so bent over in concentration that Maya could only really make out his disheveled sandy hair, with no sign of the square-jawed features that Maya never grew tired of staring at.

Their other member was working off to one side. Samit Patel was a young Asian-American tech specialist, slightly plump from too much time sitting behind computers and too little time in the field, always immaculately dressed and bespectacled. He was new to the FBI and presumably given to her because Deputy Director Harris wanted to make it clear that, just because Maya had demanded to head up the hunt for the Moonlight Killer, that didn't mean she got the best of the best.

"Samit, I have a job for you," Maya said, moving to stand in front of his desk, trying not to loom too much given that she was taller than Samit.

His neatness meant that Maya had to keep an eye on her own appearance, making sure her smart pant suits didn't have any errant coffee stains, and that her dark hair was tied back neatly from her angular features.

"Yes, Agent Gray?"

The way he said it made Maya feel so old. She was only thirty-five, but that still put her more than a decade ahead of the young tech specialist. Normally she didn't feel it, but the sense of having someone looking to her as an authority figure only helped to reinforce it.

"I have information about the kidnapper," she said. "One of his victims told me that he has a tattoo: a snake eating an armadillo under a full moon."

“That sounds pretty specific,” Samit said. Maya saw him frown. “I don’t remember that detail being in any of the reports.”

“The victim told it to me directly, and it hasn’t made it into one of my reports yet,” Maya replied. She tried to make it sound like an administrative oversight rather than a deliberate choice, made so that Harris and those around him wouldn’t put more lives at risk by organizing yet another raid on wherever they thought the kidnapper was.

If they were going to try to catch him, they had to be certain. Maya’s sister Megan was one of his hostages, and he had already hurt her once when they had gone after him, conducting a raid on an empty building. Another of his hostages had lost a finger after another raid, while a third had died trying to escape. They had to be cautious now. They couldn’t just throw themselves into the hunt for him blindly.

“OK,” Samit said, “I’ll get right on it. Although it could take a while. There are a *lot* of tattoo places out there.”

“I’d start by seeing if it has some significance,” Maya suggested. “A tattoo like that might be a gang symbol, something linked to a military unit, or something similar. But yes, failing that, you’re going to have to work your way through the portfolios of different tattoo artists, one by one. Sorry.”

She saw the tech specialist shake his head. “No, it’s not a problem. Compared to rooting through the emails of a cartel, or someone’s entire corporate system, this should be doable.”

Maya could only admire his optimism, but at least it meant that someone was working on the one direct link they had that might lead back to the Moonlight Killer. Her sister had taken a considerable risk to get this piece of information out to her. Maya had a responsibility to make sure that it translated into something much more concrete.

She went over to Marco, because the two of them had to focus on the other aspects, at least for a while. He looked up at Maya, offering her a smile as she approached.

“And there I was thinking that working for the FBI would get me away from wading through files, looking for connections.”

“You’re not regretting signing up for this, are you?” Maya asked. Marco was there on a transfer from the Cleveland PD, and the last thing Maya wanted was for him to regret the decision. She appreciated having him here. She *liked* having him here.

"No," Marco said, and he sounded definite about it. "I know that what I'm doing here has the potential to save lives, and could catch us one of the worst serial killers out there."

Maya shot a pointed look across to where Samit sat, trying to remind Marco that the new young tech didn't know what the two of them knew: that the kidnapper was actually the Moonlight Killer.

"Assuming any of the cases lead us to him," Maya said, trying to make it sound as though they were still working on the theory that the kidnapper was trying to hunt down the Moonlight Killer through his crimes, rather than knowing that he was behind all of this. It was another thing that was better to leave out of her reports to Harris, at least for now.

"It's still worth looking," Marco replied, obviously getting it. Samit was new to the team, and as helpful as he was, it was still better to keep this particular piece of information between the two of them, at least for now.

"Do you have anything on the artist who was kidnapped?" Maya asked.

"I'm still working on it," Marco said. "I have a name, Tori Blauer, and a few links to her art portfolio and social media. She was young, studied art in college, and someone snatched her from just outside what was going to be her first big art show."

"Anyone new popped up in her social media recently?" Maya asked. That seemed like a possibility. The Moonlight Killer had to be selecting his victims somehow. Was it possible that he was hunting for them online, until he found exactly what he was looking for in a potential victim?

"No one obvious," Marco said. "No new friends or followers who don't seem to be someone from her normal life. My guess is that our kidnapper isn't going to be quite that obvious about it."

Maya had to admit that Marco had a point. The Moonlight Killer was good at covering his tracks, good at leaving no traces. They'd rescued multiple women now, and they still only had the most minimal details about him. Even half the details they'd thought they'd discovered had turned out to be planted by the serial killer, arranged so that his captives would remember them rather than anything that might actually lead back to him.

Yet they still had to try to find a way to him; one that wouldn't be obvious, and wouldn't give him an excuse to hurt any more of the women who sat as his prisoners.

Maya took a seat beside Marco, trying to ignore how close that put her to him. They had to keep this professional. They were here to do a job, and try to save lives. To do that, they had to focus on the work, and not on one another.

She forced herself to focus on the files on his computer screen instead. Marco had files on the women they knew were the Moonlight Killer's prisoners open on the screen, so that he could go from one to another, trying to find any point of connection between them all.

Maya knew their names and their pasts almost by heart by now. Liza, Gabi, Katya, Carmel. Her sister, Megan. And now this young artist, Tori.

Back at the start of this, Maya had been convinced that the kidnapper was targeting young women with artistic ambitions, because of Liza Carty and Megan. Slowly, it had become clear that not every captured woman met that criterion, leaving Maya looking for some other hint of connection between them.

They had all obviously been vulnerable to being taken, but not in the same ways. While it seemed that most of those in the files had no families left or limited contact with the families they had, it wasn't true for all of them. A pattern that only fit *most* of the victims wasn't a pattern.

"Can you see any connections between them?" Maya asked Marco.

"Only the one you found before: that they look similar."

There was that. While the young women had many physical differences in terms of hair color and skin tone, they were all women in their twenties, all slightly built, with delicate features. Maybe that was enough of a similarity for the Moonlight Killer. Maybe that was all he needed in order to select a victim.

The only problem was that something about it didn't ring quite true.

"Maybe that physical similarity is a part of it," Maya said, "but it can't be the whole thing, because it doesn't do anything to explain why he picked them rather than someone else, or why he seems to have gone to so much trouble to kidnap Tori Blauer."

"I could run the files through some different analyses to see if any deeper connections show up," Samit suggested from across the office. "Maybe there *are* patterns, but ones only a computer might pick up."

"Are you suggesting that he *picks* them by computer, too?" Maya asked. "Wouldn't it take that, if it requires one to spot the pattern?"

She was glad their new tech was trying to be helpful, but in this instance it didn't feel like something that advanced their case much.

"It could be a pattern that makes sense to him, but is too complex for us," Samit suggested.

"Maybe," Maya replied. "And if it won't cost you too much time, then do it, but I want most of your attention on the tattoo."

The truth was that she suspected the Moonlight Killer wasn't selecting his victims through some complex algorithm. Serial killers didn't. It was about what felt right to them, about what fit with the pathology that they'd developed over years. Understanding more about it wasn't about some hidden quality, but about something that the Moonlight Killer would see instantly.

Maya stared at the screen, trying to see what he saw, trying to pick out what it was about these women that made them into his targets. She stared, and it seemed as if she were banging her head against a wall, making no progress.

Then something shifted, and the answer seemed so obvious that it might have been written there in large letters on the screen for her to read out. She smiled over at Marco, and he cocked his head to the side.

"You have something, don't you?"

"I think I know what the connection is."

"And?" he asked.

"All of these women, young women. All of them were standing right on the verge of something major changing in their lives. Liza Carty was just about to hit the big time with her singing. Carmel Johnson was trying to change her life after years on the street. Now Tori Blauer has been taken, just as she was about to begin her art career. He takes them right as they're on the brink of becoming something new."

Marco stared at the screen beside her, and Maya saw Samit move in as well to look.

"I think you're right," Marco said. "All of them, they were all changing in some way. All getting their lives on track, or moving onto something bigger. I think you've found it, Maya."

Maya felt a moment of pride at hearing that. She particularly liked that the validation was coming from Marco. The only question now was what they were going to do with the insight. It told them a little more about the Moonlight Killer, might even start to explain some of his old crimes, but she wasn't sure how it could lead them to him. It wasn't the kind of thing that could provide their little team with a location, or even help to identify his next potential victim so that they could be waiting.

For the moment, it felt as if they were still at the Moonlight Killer's mercy, forced to react, forced to simply wait until he decided to send them another case to solve. Maya hated that fact, hated having to sit and wait while her sister was in danger somewhere, in the hands of a killer.

Maya was still thinking about how *much* she hated it when the door opened, revealing Agent Reyes, her colleague on the fourth floor and also Deputy Director Harris's go-to guy in recent weeks. The young Latino agent was too ambitious for Maya's taste, and too quick to try to grab the kidnapper, whatever the cost. Even so, she couldn't deny that he was an effective agent.

"What is it, Reyes?" she asked.

"Harris wants to see you," Reyes said. He seemed to be enjoying it. "He wants to know why you haven't made any progress yet."

CHAPTER THREE

The man they called Frank was burying a body in the woods.

It wasn't something he had a lot of experience with, strangely. When he killed, he preferred to leave the aftermath for others to find. He killed and he left the bodies in the place where he'd murdered his victims.

That was a part of what he did, the discovery a part of the purpose of his work, so that people had the potential to see the message in it. Not that they ever did. That was simply a part of the inferiority of most people.

This wasn't one of his kills, though. Haley Dennison had done this to herself. She'd found a sharp enough edge to slash her own wrists while still in her cage, where she should have been safe, where she should have been contained.

His former bunny had found a way to cheat Frank, to take herself out of his carefully prepared plan, to create a hole where there shouldn't be one. He had to have twelve bunnies. Twelve was the number. Twelve was the *point*.

Most of the time, Frank could have walked along any street in the country without anyone guessing who or what he was. He was of only slightly more than average height, with dark hair and blue-gray eyes, and features that most people would have found handsome under other circumstances. Even if he was dressed in simple dark clothes, most people wouldn't have suspected anything sinister about him.

Not today, though. Not with a cold, killing fury consuming his features as he dug the hole that would contain Haley Dennison's body. This was the second bunny he'd lost in the last couple of weeks, both to their own stupidity. This one had killed herself, and Carmel had tried to escape, leaving him with no choice but to end her.

Neither of them seemed to have thought for an instant about the impact their choices would have on him. About the trouble that it would cause for him. Hadn't he told them all that this was part of a larger plan? That they would be released if Maya solved the problems that he set for her? Hadn't he told them that there were rules to this game? Rules that they must all follow?

He set his booted foot against Haley's body and rolled it down into the hole with a grunt of effort.

They'd both broken the rules, in their own ways. It had cost both of them their lives, but that hardly made things easier for Frank. It meant that he had to do this, for one thing, starting to fill in the hole with his shovel while the daylight poured down through the canopy of the trees. The area was isolated, but even so, it was a risk.

He finished filling in the grave, patting down the soil and then selecting surrounding foliage to disguise the spot. He picked branches with thorns deliberately, making sure to arrange them in such a way as to deter any animals that might try to dig for the bones. That would cause too many problems.

Frank took a moment to survey his work. There was no hint of satisfaction at a job well done. This whole thing was a mess, barely contained. It only added to his fury.

He stalked home through the woods, taking a circuitous route so that even in the unlikely event a passing hunter or hiker spotted him, they wouldn't be able to link him to the spot where he'd buried the body. He didn't want to have to add another death to today's tally, not when it wasn't planned, wasn't a *part* of the plan.

The plan was everything, for him and for Maya Gray. Even if she couldn't quite see the whole of it yet, she was as bound up in it now as a fly in a spider's web.

Frank guessed he should be grateful that it had been one of the other bunnies who had killed herself, and not Maya's sister, Megan. *That* might have thrown the whole business into disarray. Just the thought of something that serious happening sent a rare note of near panic fluttering in Frank's chest.

It made him hurry back to his cabin. From the outside, it was a bucolic scene, set in the middle of a flower-strewn clearing where bunnies of a more literal kind than the ones he'd collected hopped and played. The cabin itself was large and custom built with two stories above ground, a balcony from which Frank could look out over the surrounding woodland, and carefully hidden cameras that looked out rather more effectively.

Frank headed back inside, among the handmade furniture, the carefully woven rugs, and the small number of hunting trophies on the walls. He stood there for several seconds, trying to calm himself, but there was too much to be done right then to waste time like that.

He headed for the trapdoor leading down to his bunker. He paused in the anteroom to pull on his mask and gloves. He already had a knife and gun stuffed into his belt, so he didn't bother with the stun gun lying on a shelf at the side. He didn't bother with grabbing food for his bunnies either. He was in no mood to waste time with them today.

He unlocked the large metal door leading to the rest of the underground bunker. Strip lights flickered overhead in the network of tunnels he'd had built there. On another occasion, his bunnies might have been wandering those tunnels freely, but Frank had kept them in their hutches since the death of one of their number.

They were huddled there, each of them alone now, locked in her cage. There should have been eight of them again now that he had kidnapped Tori Blauer, but instead, only seven faces looked back, thanks to Haley Dennison's efforts.

They looked on with fear, all of them so delicate and fragile, all of them exactly the type that he might have chosen for his… other work. It made the whole thing a little more straightforward.

Except that none of this was straightforward. Oh, dear Maya was doing an admirable job, but the rest of it… there were more unexpected variables than he had anticipated. He prided himself for staying in control of situations, for knowing more, for planning more, yet now, things had gone well beyond his plans.

That angered Frank considerably.

"Are you going to keep us in these cages forever?" Megan Gray asked, from within her hutch.

Frank whirled toward her, and through the holes in his mask, the coldness of his eyes fixed on her, making her take a step back. She was afraid of him. That was good. That was as things should be. He'd beaten her precisely, exactly, for her sister's missteps. That had left her frightened of him.

Yet, even as he thought that, Frank saw Megan steel herself and stand up, facing him with a note of defiance. Frank started to lash out, and only stopped himself with an effort, reminding himself just how much he needed this particular bunny. All of them.

He needed more. *One* more, to be precise.

"You'll stay in your hutches until I can be sure you won't do anything stupid," Frank snarled. "I tried to give you freedom to roam. I tried to look after you, my bunnies, but you rejected my kindness. Two of your number have broken my rules. I won't let that happen again."

He turned on his heel and headed toward the control room at the heart of his bunker, leaving his bunnies where they were. Perhaps later, he would bring himself to be charming and entertaining with them again, to feed them and care for them as he knew he had to if all of this was going to work. For now, though, he had more important matters to attend to.

He went through another locked door, into a large, circular room. One space in it was clear, with a drain set in the floor and a hook above, for use if it became necessary to kill any of the women he was holding. It was best to be prepared for such things.

More of the room was given over to a bank of screens, showing information flowing in from around the country. None of the video feeds showed Maya Gray, but the audio tap on her phone was there, waiting for anything that might help him. Frank was thorough when it came to surveillance.

He sat in the large leather chair that stood in front of those screens, ripping off his mask and tossing it to one side in frustration. That frustration was for a simple reason:

He didn't know what to do next.

Or rather, he didn't have every detail of it mapped out. In general terms, of course, Frank understood *exactly* what he needed to do: he needed to replace Haley Dennison. Yet he didn't have the precise method by which he would do so planned yet. He had only just used his contingency plan for the loss of one of his bunnies in finding Tori Blauer. To have to find another, so soon after acquiring her?

It was an additional complication that Frank did not need.

He began by scouring the internet for a suitable new bunny. The basic criteria were easy enough: female, the right age, the right appearance. If those had been the only boxes to tick, Frank wouldn't have needed to be so careful about what he did.

The next part was harder, looking for someone who fit the more important criterion of being just on the cusp of changing her life. People tended to announce things on social media only *after* the big moment had come, so Frank had to work harder to find suitable targets.

Even then, he wasn't done. It wasn't enough for a potential victim to be suitable; she also had to be vulnerable. *Particularly* for this. In some ways, kidnapping was far more difficult than killing might have been. To kill, Frank only needed a brief time when his victim would be alone. A successful kidnapping required more planning. It required an entire exit strategy that would make it seem as if the young woman in question had simply disappeared. Ideally, it required a victim who wouldn't be missed immediately, buying time for her transportation before the police started looking for her.

Finding all of that took work, but Frank was used to that work, and he was able to narrow down the possibilities considerably, a series of photographs sitting on his screen. One face stood out to him, young and blonde-haired, with a particularly winning smile. Claire Rainford.

"You," Frank decided. "It will be you."

He'd learned to listen to his instincts in such matters a long time ago. Certainly, he'd never tried to deny such impulses.

The only problem now was setting the kidnapping up. Frank had already found out the hard way that he couldn't do that and watch his bunnies adequately. If he gave Claire his full attention, then who was to say that another of his bunnies might not find a way to spoil things?

Besides, he needed to monitor things with Maya, and to do that properly, he needed to be here.

That meant, for the set-up to the kidnapping, Frank would have to enlist help. He didn't mind doing that, of course. He had a small network of people he either employed or controlled, helping him with everything from delivering postcards to murdering prison inmates. But this was the kind of thing that he normally liked to do himself.

It couldn't be helped, though. He would have to call in assistance for this part of things. He was too busy for anything else. He had to be here to watch over things, and to follow dear Maya's progress.

Especially when he'd picked out the *perfect* case for her to look into next.

CHAPTER FOUR

Maya actually felt nervous as she stood outside Deputy Director Harris's office. She found her weight shifting nervously, and had to tell herself that this was nothing to worry about. She had everything in hand.

Part of the nerves came from the other figures in the room with Harris. Her boss sat behind his desk, looking as avuncular as always with his shaven head, faint smile, and open features. He wore an open-necked shirt and a sports jacket.

The woman to his left caught Maya's attention, because Maya was sure that she'd seen her before. She was probably in her late forties, with blonde hair tied back severely and deliberately understated makeup and sharp features that didn't seem to have any give to them.

It took a moment for Maya to realize exactly where she'd seen this woman before: this was Judith Swift, of the BAU, the woman who had led the team trying to catch the Moonlight Killer for years. Maya had seen her face when she'd been looking at old files on the cases.

She knew the face of the man to Harris's right without having to hesitate. He was probably in his fifties, square-jawed and stern-faced, with graying hair, but clean shaven. He had a flag pin in his lapel, and a pen balanced between the fingers of two spade-like hands.

Director Adams, Harris's boss, was in the room.

Where normally Maya would have been happy that Harris was taking an interest in what she was doing, *this* level of interest was something else entirely. To have two other such senior figures here on the fourth floor suggested that something worrying was happening here.

"Come in," Harris called out, obviously seeing Maya waiting.

She stepped inside. There was no chair in front of Harris's desk today; presumably one of the others beside him had it. It meant that Maya had to stand in front of the three of them like a soldier facing a court-martial, and she had to resist the old instinct to stand at attention. She wasn't in the army now. This was the FBI, and Maya had the confidence that she was good at her job.

"Gray, this is Director Adams and Agent Swift. They're here to hear about the kidnapping case."

He made it sound as if it were a normal thing, rather than something that almost never happened. The director of the FBI was normally more interested in budgets and strategic priorities, liaising with the President himself and with the deputy directors in charge of particular departments. He didn't get involved in cases.

Yet here he was, in front of Maya.

"What would you like to know?" Maya asked.

Director Adams answered that. "Why don't you start from the beginning with this case? Tell me where you're up to?"

Maya did her best. "Several weeks ago, I received a postcard claiming that a kidnapper had taken twelve women hostage, including my missing sister, Megan. To secure the release of the women, he has demanded that I solve cold cases he directs me to, with each successful resolution leading to the release of one of the women. So far, I have been able to secure the release of four women."

"And all of these cases have related to the Moonlight Killer in some way?" Agent Swift asked. Maya could hear something close to hunger in her tone.

Maya knew how dangerous the next few moments could be for her. She couldn't just come out and say that it was the Moonlight Killer sending her these cases to work through, because that would reveal just how much she'd been holding back from Deputy Director Harris. It would get her thrown off the case at least, probably fired, maybe arrested.

If that happened, she wouldn't be able to help her sister, and the fear of that forced Maya to be careful about what she said next.

"Strictly speaking, none of them have," Maya replied. "The cases have all proven to be the work of other killers, believed to be the Moonlight Killer's work either because local law enforcement saw a tenuous link, or because the actual killer sought to disguise their work as his."

"So the kidnapper has you chasing the Moonlight Killer, but you keep striking out?" Agent Swift asked.

Maya reined in a sudden flash of annoyance. This wasn't somewhere that she could afford to speak out of turn.

"With respect, I have been succeeding, because I've found the people who really committed the murders I've been sent to investigate."

"No one is doubting that you have brought killers to justice, Agent Gray," Director Adams said. "I think Agent Swift would like to know if you think your investigation will eventually lead you to the Moonlight Killer."

Again, Maya was only too aware of just how carefully she had to answer that question. She didn't want to lie outright, but she couldn't give the people in this room the whole picture.

"I think there's a very real chance that it will," Maya said.

She saw Agent Swift look across to Harris. "Then this investigation should be folded into my team's efforts. Agent Gray is doing a good job, but my team has been working on finding the Moonlight Killer for—"

"That is not my primary focus," Maya cut in. She didn't want to be folded into anyone's team, not when getting her own tiny task force had taken so much effort. "It is possible that the investigation might give us the Moonlight Killer, and if it does, I will be happy to share information, but my primary focus is on securing the safe release of the hostages."

Harris nodded at that. "On that front, what progress have you made?"

Maya frowned. Harris knew exactly what progress she'd made, because he'd been there for most of it. "Sir, I've secured the release of four women."

"That's not what I mean and you know it, Gray," he said. "What progress have you made in finding the kidnapper who took them?"

"I have Patel and Detective Spinelli checking leads now," Maya replied. It was a noncommittal answer, and she knew it.

"Ah, yes, Detective Spinelli," Director Adams said. "Tell me, why are you working with"—he looked down, obviously checking a note—"a detective on secondment from the Cleveland Police Department, rather than with trained FBI agents?"

"Detective Spinelli proved instrumental in helping me to crack the first case," Maya said, "and his assistance has been invaluable since."

"But you still haven't made headway on catching the bastard who is behind all this," Harris snapped.

Maya knew that she should keep things professional, but she also knew that if she didn't do anything to defend the way she was going about things, there was a risk that her recently founded taskforce would simply be taken out of her hands. Harris was obviously having second thoughts about going along with it, and why not, when Maya had pretty much forced him into it?

"Every case we work gives us more information on him," Maya said. "But we've already seen the dangers of trying to act on that information too soon, sir. The raids we've conducted in the past haven't gotten us close to the kidnapper, but *have* led to him hurting the hostages. For now, the best way to make progress is to solve the cases that we're sent, and secure the release of more women."

"That is a long way from being a proactive strategy, Agent Gray," Agent Swift pointed out.

"But it's working," Maya shot back. She couldn't afford to just be on the defensive with this. "I've also solved a number of cases that your department seems to have labeled as the Moonlight Killer's work and then left."

She saw the flicker of anger on the other woman's face at that. No one liked being reminded that they weren't succeeding at their job.

"And gotten one woman killed, from what I hear."

"Carmel Johnson died trying to escape the kidnapper," Maya said. "Her death couldn't be prevented."

"As I understand it, we only have the kidnapper's word for that, Agent Gray," Director Adams said. "This is a very serious matter. I wouldn't be involved if it weren't, and it seems that our primary strategy is to sit back and allow a kidnapper to dictate terms. That goes against everything the FBI does in hostage situations. We don't negotiate with these people, Agent Gray. We don't give in to threats."

Maya knew the FBI playbook as well as he did. The problem was that the Moonlight Killer also seemed to know exactly what they would and wouldn't do in any situation.

"Deputy Director Harris has given me the freedom to run my taskforce how I see fit, sir," Maya said. "The kidnapper will only communicate with me, which means that I am uniquely placed in all of this."

"As I understand it, you essentially threatened to withdraw all assistance if there were any more raids," Director Adams said. "As I said, Agent Gray, we are not in the habit of giving in to threats."

Maya realized then that she might have overstepped. She'd been pushed into a position where she'd had to force Harris's hand, just to protect her sister, but in doing so, she'd made enemies she couldn't afford to have.

"I still believe that this is the most effective way to resolve this, sir," she told the director. "I wouldn't have pushed so hard for this if I didn't believe it was the best possible way to try to preserve lives and eventually catch the kidnapper."

"But one woman is dead," Harris put in, "and the kidnapper could choose to kill the rest any time he wants."

Maya was about to point out that his own approach hadn't exactly done anything to resolve things when Agent Swift cut in.

"What if you fail?" she asked.

Maya looked over at her. "I'm sorry?"

"As I understand it, the release of these hostages is predicated on you successfully solving cold cases." Agent Swift spread her hands. "I'm not denying that you've been successful so far, but what happens if you run into a case you can't solve, or can't solve in time?"

Then a woman would die for it, maybe even her sister. Maya had known that from the very start of this. It was that possibility that made her push so hard when she was working on the cold cases. She had to succeed, because the alternative was too awful to contemplate.

"I can't afford to fail," Maya said. "Which is exactly why I can't be distracted by trying to conduct some kind of parallel investigation into the kidnapper, jumping at every possible lead and walking into the traps he sets because of that."

She said that with a pointed look Harris's way. He'd obviously set all of this up as a way of trying to go back on everything he'd allowed her to do. He wouldn't close down the taskforce himself, but he might allow his superior to do it. Maya needed to remind him again that his way of doing things had only put lives at risk. Multiple times now, they'd tried to raid locations based on information that they'd thought would lead them to the kidnapper, and every time, they'd found that the Moonlight Killer had been a step ahead of them, leading them to empty buildings, setting traps ahead of them, and then punishing the women he held for it.

Maya had photographs of every bruise he'd inflicted on her sister for one of the raids. She couldn't allow it to happen again.

"I am aware that previous attempts haven't gone well," Director Adams said. "And I am not advocating any more of these premature raids. Yet I do think that a more… immediate resolution than simply waiting for this man to play out his twisted game is required. If you can provide that, Agent Gray, then I am happy for your taskforce to continue. If not…"

He left that hanging, and Maya struggled to think of something to say in response. What *could* she say to the threat of being taken off the case, of having no way to save her sister?

Maya was still trying to think of something when an agent knocked on the door and entered without waiting for an answer.

"What is it?" Harris asked. "Can't you see we're in a meeting?"

"I'm sorry, sir, but this just arrived anonymously for Agent Gray."

He held something up, and Maya's heart leapt into her mouth at the sight of another postcard sitting there in the agent's hand, gamboling bunny rabbits carefully penned on the front by the Moonlight Killer.

Maya knew what it had to mean: he had another case for her.

CHAPTER FIVE

Maya grabbed the postcard from the agent's hand, running with it back toward the office she shared with her team. She wasn't worried about forensics from the postcard right then, because that had already been shown with previous cards to be a dead end. She was just interested in getting started as quickly as possible.

"Gray!" Harris called after her.

"No time, sir!" Maya called back. "The clock is ticking!"

In truth, she was grateful for the excuse to be out of that meeting. Thankfully, superiors or not, murder took priority. Maya needed every second she could get on this. As Agent Swift had so pointedly reminded her, if she failed, then a woman was going to die.

Maya read the postcard as she burst into the office, setting it down in front of Marco.

"We have another postcard!"

Dear Maya,

You have done quite well, so far. Let's see how you do with this: Amber Kaley, of Philadelphia. You have until midnight on the 13th. I have every confidence in you.

That was only two days away, the shortest deadline Maya had yet been given for one of these cases. Almost impossibly short. Was it even possible to conduct a full investigation in two days?

"Marco, we need to get to Philadelphia. Samit, can you send over the files for the case to me? Better yet, call me with the details while we're en route."

Maya had taken to keeping a bag with a change of clothes and toiletries at the office, precisely because of the need to move quickly if something like this happened. She grabbed it and was pleased to see that Marco was already on his feet, heading for the door.

"It will take us a couple of hours to get to Philadelphia," he said. "I'll drive."

They practically ran through the office. Harris was out there in the bullpen, with Director Adams standing beside him.

"Gray, what's happening?"

"Another case, sir," Maya said, without stopping. "Sorry, no time to brief you. The deadline is only two days this time. Patel will give you the details."

She was already in an elevator with Marco before her boss could answer. Maya guessed that was a good thing. She definitely didn't want the complication of having to explain things to Harris, or the delay that would come from it.

She and Marco hurried down into the FBI's parking garage, practically leaping into Betsy, Marco's beaten-up old Explorer. Maya knew from experience that it was a lot faster than it looked, and today, she was grateful for that. She would need every minute in order to have a chance of solving this.

"Two days isn't a lot," Marco said, as he started to race out through the streets of the capital, lights flashing to keep other cars out of the way. He wasn't quite driving at pursuit speeds, but he was definitely over the speed limit, obviously trying to make up as much time for Maya as possible.

"It's less than he's given me before," Maya said. "I hope that means it's a simple case."

"What's the alternative?"

"That he *wants* me to fail." Just saying those words brought a sinking feeling of dread that sat in the pit of Maya's stomach. Was it possible that the Moonlight Killer was deliberately making this one more difficult so that he would have an excuse to kill one of his hostages? Had he decided that he simply wanted to hurt Maya like that now?

It was entirely possible. It wasn't as if Maya could exactly complain that a serial killer wasn't being fair.

"I don't think that's what he wants," Marco said. "He wants you to clear up cases that are misattributed to him, and he obviously has more to come. He can't keep you doing what he wants if you know he's going to make it impossible for you to win his little games."

Maya hoped that was true. Nevertheless, she couldn't shake the feeling that this was all some kind of ruse, some kind of way of letting him hurt Megan while claiming that it was her fault.

Maya hated the feeling that came with that: the sensation of being utterly helpless in the face of whatever the Moonlight Killer might choose to do. Maya was doing her best to play along with the rules of his game, and had even managed to stop her boss from spending all his time trying to catch the kidnapper rather than solve the cases he set and save the women.

Yet all of that might be for nothing, and that thought made Maya shiver. She hated the thought that she couldn't do anything, couldn't change anything. She had no control over the time that she'd been given. What if it really wasn't enough time to do what she'd been sent to do?

Maya felt Marco's hand close over hers. "It will be all right, Maya. You're amazing at your job. I've never seen anyone close cold cases the way you do. If anyone can close a case like this in two days, it's you."

Maya needed to feel the pressure of his hand on hers right then. She needed that reassurance, and it helped a lot that it was coming from Marco. There was something electric about that contact, a spark between them that had Maya looking over at him, taking in the lightly unshaven line of his jaw and his slightly disheveled hair.

A part of her wanted to reach out to touch that hair, to be closer to him. Maya could smell the scent of him so close to her, a masculine scent with just a touch of sweat. It was impossible to deny just how attracted Maya felt to Marco when they were both in such close proximity to one another.

He glanced over, and for a moment, their eyes seemed to catch on one another's, so that they were staring, the moment stretching…

The blare of a horn snapped them both out of it, as Marco put his full attention back on driving, sliding in and out of traffic with ease as they made their way northeast along the coast, out of the greater DC area, heading toward the smaller sprawl of Philadelphia.

Maya knew she shouldn't keep staring at Marco, but she couldn't help it. Working together meant that the two of them spent more time together than ever, but honestly, Maya would have liked even more than that. The urge to reach out and touch him again was still there.

Maya suppressed that urge, for two reasons. The first was a simple one: she didn't want to risk distracting Marco again while he was driving so fast, taking them along the coast, with the Atlantic visible in the distance through the passenger window of the Explorer. He was trying to save them every minute he could with his driving, and that meant they were moving at the kind of speed where they couldn't afford any distractions.

Maya couldn't afford any distractions in general right then, and that was the second reason why she held back. She was working with Marco now, and Maya needed that working relationship to go smoothly if she was going to save the remaining women the Moonlight Killer held; if she was going to save her sister.

She couldn't afford to complicate that with anything between her and Marco, no matter how much her instincts told her that she should, no matter what kind of attraction she felt toward him just then. She only had two days to solve a murder. It didn't leave any time for anything else, certainly not for anything that might prove as distracting as Marco promised to be.

She had to focus on the case, had to make use of every moment over the next couple of days to try to find a killer in time.

With that in mind, Maya got out her phone and called Samit, who answered after three or four rings. Since the Moonlight Killer would undoubtedly be listening in, it felt a little like confirming to the serial killer that she was actually making a serious effort with the case. She put the phone on speaker, so that Marco would be able to hear.

"Agent Gray?" Samit said.

"Samit, how are things going with the case files?"

"I've sent a copy over to your internal email," Samit said, "so you should be able to access everything you need electronically."

"Great," Maya replied. "Now, give me the basics."

"The basics?"

Maya had to remind herself that Samit was inexperienced, even if he was supposedly very good at what he did as a tech.

"Tell us about the case," Marco said.

Maya could only agree with that sentiment. "Summarize the file for me, Samit. Tell me about the victim, and about what happened."

"OK, no problem," Samit said. There was a brief pause on the other end of the line, presumably as he started to read the file. "Amber Kaley, twenty-seven. Lived at an address on Cypress Street, Philadelphia. Killed by a single stab wound while out jogging after work, on August twenty-third last year."

"Can you check for me if the twenty-third of August was the night of the full moon?" Maya asked.

Another pause, and Maya found herself willing the tech to hurry up. She knew it took time to look the fact up, but she was painfully aware of every moment that passed.

"You think it will have been?" Marco asked.

"Yes," Samit replied. "I can confirm that the twenty-third was a full moon."

"Which is probably why the local PD decided it was the Moonlight Killer," Maya said.

"There has to be another reason," Marco put in. "Not every murder on the full moon is down to the Moonlight Killer, and there's no reason for a local department to just assume it."

That was a good point.

"Samit," Maya asked, "is there any sign of *why* the Philadelphia PD thought that this might be the Moonlight Killer?"

"Looking at the file, it seems that they had a few initial suspects, but those lines of inquiry fell through pretty quickly. There was no sign of it being a robbery, no initial sign that Amber Kaley had any obvious enemies. The killing seemed to come out of nowhere. Combine that with the night of the full moon, and…"

And the Moonlight Killer had been a convenient boogeyman on which to pin the death.

It seemed that Samit wasn't done, though. "There is a note in our files that Agent Swift's unit looked at the case, but didn't follow it up."

He'd found out more than Maya had asked for, which was at least a little impressive. Maya wasn't surprised that Agent Swift and those who worked with her had dismissed the case being one of the Moonlight Killer's: he strangled his victims rather than stabbing them.

Of course, Maya had far better reasons for believing that it wasn't his work: that was the whole reason that he sent her to investigate these cases, trying to find out the truth and clear his name, as if he didn't want his own collection of murders tainted by anyone else's work.

"Where did the victim work?" Maya asked.

"She was a nurse at the university hospital there," Samit said.

"Family?" Marco asked.

"A sister and her parents. I can find addresses for them."

"Do that," Maya said. It was good to have this level of support, without having to beg other agents for favors or rely on help from the local police department. "One other thing, I need to know exactly where the murder took place. I want to look at things on the ground."

"I'll send across the address," Samit said.

"Thanks," Maya replied, and hung up. She looked over to Marco. "What do you think?"

"Well, we know it isn't the Moonlight Killer," he said.

They could agree on that much, at least.

"The question is where we start to find a way into this, if the local PD ran down all the leads."

"True," Maya said. It was a worrying thought. "I'm going to go through the files, hope there's something in there that got missed the first time around."

She pulled up the files on her phone, starting to read while outside the freeway continued to flash past.

Maya just hoped that when they got to Philadelphia, they would find something on the ground that would let them find the killer quickly. With such a short deadline, they couldn't afford to get anything wrong.

CHAPTER SIX

As Maya and Marco made their way through the streets of Philadelphia, driving toward the spot where Amber Kaley had been murdered, Maya found herself looking around, trying to get some sense of the area where Amber had been killed.

The skyscrapers of the city rose up around her, historic buildings dotted between them in a strange interplay between old and new, carefully up to date and slightly run-down. Maya could see a heart to the city of rising, gleaming buildings, surrounded by a more industrial, older spread of buildings around them, with the Delaware and Schuylkill Rivers cutting through its heart.

They headed for the heart of the city. Amber had been murdered on the edge of the Schuylkill River Park, so that was the spot Maya needed to see. The two of them pulled up outside of the large, open green space, with its view out onto the river beyond, and Maya sat there for a moment or two, trying to get a sense of where Amber would have come from to get here.

"Are we going to check in with local PD now that we're in town?" Marco asked.

It was an important question. Typically, Maya would have done exactly that. She *had* done that on her previous cases. Yet now, she found herself feeling ambivalent. She'd definitely had somc help from local departments—Marco wouldn't be here with her if that weren't the case—but Maya had also faced obstruction, and even outright hostility.

Local police departments didn't like being told that they were wrong about focusing on the Moonlight Killer, and with only two days to find the real answer, Maya didn't have any time to spare dealing with the kind of harassment and outright sabotage that she'd run into before.

"I'll call to let them know we're here," Maya said. "But now that we have a formal taskforce, we don't have to rely on the local PD for resources, and I can't take the chance that they'll want to get in the way."

Marco looked a little concerned as Maya said that.

"There's a risk that you'll alienate the local police by doing that," he pointed out. "They'll see it as the FBI sweeping into town and trying to take over."

"I'm going to call them," Maya assured him. "I'm going to do everything I can to make sure that they're OK with this, but ultimately… we're in town for two days. We don't have enough time to risk getting caught up going back and forth with the local police, and we have enough resources of our own to do this without their help."

Still, Marco looked doubtful.

"I'll call them now," Maya told him. "It will be fine."

At least, she hoped it would be fine. The last thing she needed was the kind of obstruction she'd faced in, for example, Louisiana, where she and Marco had found themselves arrested after the local sheriff falsely claimed that their rental car was stolen.

"I'll make the call," Maya said. "You take a look around, try to see if there's anything about the location that makes it obvious why someone would choose to kill here."

Marco nodded and got out of the car, leaving Maya there.

She took out her phone. Normally, she left this part to Harris, but now that she was the head of her own small taskforce, Maya guessed that this part fell to her. She found the number for the Philadelphia PD's main switchboard and called it.

"Philadelphia Police Department, how may I direct your call?"

"This is Agent Maya Gray with the FBI. I'd like to talk to the detective in charge of the Amber Kaley murder, please."

"Please hold."

Maya wanted to say that she didn't have enough time to hold. She certainly hated sitting there in the car, watching Marco move around the riverside park freely while she was stuck there in the car listening to the Philadelphia PD's taste in elevator jazz. She wanted to be out there doing useful work, work that might actually lead her to the killer. About the only thing that made it better was the fact that it was Marco she was watching, and Maya could have stared at the detective all day.

Even that wasn't completely satisfying, though, not when she'd already told herself she couldn't afford that kind of complication right now.

Finally, the music clicked off.

"This is Detective Ian Tanner," a gruff voice on the other end of the line said. "Am I speaking to Agent Gray?"

"That's me," Maya said. "I'm currently in town, heading up a taskforce that has been tasked with looking into this murder as part of a broader inquiry."

"The FBI is in town again?" Detective Tanner said. "You're here looking for the Moonlight Killer?"

Ultimately, of course, that was the point of Maya's little taskforce. He was the kidnapper. He was the one who would ultimately pay for all of this. Right then, though, Maya couldn't afford to let slip the fact that she knew who the kidnapper was. She had to play this a different way.

"This is in connection to another, related, case," Maya explained. "A series of kidnappings, where the kidnapper appears to have a fascination with the Moonlight Killer's crimes. As part of that investigation, I need to look into Amber Kaley's death again."

She heard Detective Tanner sigh on the other end of the phone. "I couldn't stop you from doing that even if I wanted, could I?"

"Would you want to?" Maya countered. "I'm trying to solve a cold case here, Detective. My guess is that you don't get as much time as you'd like to investigate those, when you have a full docket of current cases to take care of."

That got another sigh from the other end of the line. "Fair enough. Even so, you've just come here without so much as a heads-up."

Maya wanted to keep being conciliatory, but she also knew that, as the head of a taskforce, she couldn't just give way on something like that. She tried to put it as politely as she could.

"That's why I'm making this courtesy call to you, Detective. I didn't have to. This is an FBI investigation. I want to keep you in the loop, and I won't bc asking for resources from your department. This is just a call to make sure that we won't be getting in one another's way. There's a time pressure on this, and I can't afford to spend that time butting heads with you."

There was silence on the other end of the line, presumably as Detective Tanner thought about his options in that regard. Maya found herself frightened in that moment that she was going to run into the kind of interference she had experienced back in Pollock, Louisiana, and without the time to absorb that kind of trouble.

Had she done the wrong thing, making this call? She and Marco could have come in, investigated, and been out of Philadelphia before anyone in the local PD realized they were even there.

But was that a realistic thought, when she was going to be interviewing people connected to Amber Kaley? If she hadn't called, then at least one of them would probably have gotten in touch with Detective Tanner at some point. She couldn't just run an investigation in secret.

"I understand," Detective Tanner said at last. "And I won't get in your way. I expect to be kept informed of anything that comes up, though. This is still my case, Agent Gray."

"Of course," Maya said, although she wasn't sure quite how much time she would actually have to report back to the local police. She certainly wasn't going to conduct the investigation hamstrung by the need to constantly check in. She hoped, though, that she would be able to at least present Detective Tanner with a closed case at the end of all this.

"I don't know what you're going to find, though," he said. "You think you're going to come up with something that we haven't?"

"I hope so," Maya said. She had to. If she didn't, then in two days, less now, a woman was going to die. Her *sister* might die. Maya had to find something that would stop that from happening.

She hung up and went out to join Marco. He was looking at his phone, and Maya guessed that Samit had sent a copy of the file across to him as well. He was standing in a spot on a trail that led through the park, in the middle of a kind of switchback, sheltered by trees.

"How were the local PD?" he asked, as Maya approached.

"They won't be giving us any trouble," she said. She hoped it was true. "Have you found anything?"

"Looking at the file, I'm pretty sure this is the spot where the murder took place," Marco said, indicating a spot a few feet in front of where he was currently standing.

Maya moved to stand there. From that spot, she couldn't see the river, couldn't see the city, couldn't even see much of the rest of the park, thanks to the surrounding trees and bushes. It was a blind spot.

More than that, it was exactly the kind of place to plan an ambush.

"The killer would have been able to see Amber coming along the path if they waited near the bend, but she wouldn't have been able to see them," Maya said. "Not until she was right on top of them. But…"

"But?" Marco said.

"But someone would have to know that she would come this way. It's not the kind of place someone waits in by chance, hoping someone will come along for them to kill."

"How would they know that she would be here?" Marco asked. "I mean, maybe she took the same route every day, but even then…"

Maya had an idea about that, though. She got out her phone, calling back to headquarters.

"Agent Gray?" Samit said, as he answered.

"I need you to find Amber Kaley's social media for me. Specifically, I need to know if she posted her regular jogging routes."

"OK," Samit said. "Give me a second."

Maya could hear the sound of keys tapping in the background.

"Yes," he replied after a minute or so. "I'm looking at an archived page now. Amber Kaley posted several public pictures of data from a GPS fitness tracker, showing pretty much the same route each time."

"A route going through Schuylkill River Park, Philadelphia?" Maya asked.

"That's right."

Which gave them at least one plausible way that Amber's killer might have known that she would have come that way.

"Thanks," Maya said, and hung up.

So they had a killer who had targeted Amber, who knew where she would be, and who had lain in wait to strike swiftly.

"Do you have the autopsy report there, Marco?" Maya asked.

She saw Marco nod, and he brought it up on his phone. "A single stab wound. No sign of drag marks on the body, or of defensive wounds."

So this was a killer who had struck suddenly, then left Amber to die where she fell. That took a kind of cold calculation, a kind of planning. It also took some kind of connection to Amber.

This hadn't been random, after all. No one planned something like this without knowing the victim, without having some kind of reason to do it. But what? That was the hard part here. With a killer who had struck out of nowhere, it was natural to react as if this were all just random, or as if there had been no reason to it, yet there had to have been, for someone to go to the trouble of setting up an ambush.

Finding that reason felt like Maya's best chance of uncovering the truth of all of this. To do that, she had to look closer at Amber Kaley's life, and she had to do it right away.

“We need to talk to Amber’s family.”

CHAPTER SEVEN

Marco drove them over to the address Maya got for Amber's family. He could practically feel the intensity of her focus as she started to work through her phone, looking at the files. At moments like this, it was as if she came to life. She was always good-looking, always an impressive, intelligent woman, but when she had a case like this, it was as if she glowed with an inner fire that drove her to get things done.

Marco had to admit, that made it kind of hard to keep his eyes on the road.

"Hello, Mrs. Kaley?" Maya asked, as she made the call to arrange this meeting. "This is Agent Maya Gray from the FBI's cold case unit. Yes, it's about your daughter. I was hoping that I could come over to speak to you. As soon as possible, if that's OK? It is, thank you."

It felt strange to Marco, already driving to see the family while still asking them for permission to do exactly that. The urgency of it all felt closer to the kind of thing Marco had experienced in live murder cases, where the standard police playbook said that the first forty-eight hours were the crucial window when it came to finding answers.

But then, they had just as little time here, and with even greater stakes. Now, it wasn't just the risk of a murderer getting away with their crimes that made everything so urgent. If they were too slow in all of this, if they failed, then a woman was probably going to die at the hands of the Moonlight Killer.

Marco would do everything he could to stop that from happening. Everything he could to help Maya find answers. He'd seen her in action: if anyone could find the truth in this, it was her.

But he'd also seen how caught up in things, how near obsessed, Maya could be. He needed to be there for her through this. She would need Marco to help keep her focused.

They pulled onto the street where Amber Kaley's family lived, in a brownstone apartment block with a large tree out front. The street felt quiet, surprisingly peaceful for an inner city, although Marco knew as well as anyone that sometimes the quietest places could hide the worst crimes.

“Are you ready to go in?” Maya asked. She was already starting to get out of the car.

Marco nodded. “Just remember that this is still a grieving family, Maya.”

The look she gave him was slightly offended.

“I’m not going to forget that,” she said, but there had been a reason Marco said it. He’d seen how driven Maya got when the time pressure on these cases got short. She was utterly driven, had so many feelings about the risk to her sister, and sometimes that meant that she forgot just how many feelings were involved for other people.

They headed up to the door and buzzed for the Kaleys’ floor.

“This is Agent Gray,” Maya said. “I’m here with my colleague, Detective Marco Spinelli.”

The door buzzed to let them in, and the pair of them made their way up a couple of flights of stairs to stand outside the family’s apartment. The door was already opening as they got there, revealing a young woman who looked too much like the photographs of Amber Kaley for her to be anyone other than her sister. She was tall and slender, with long dark hair tied back in a braid, dark eyes, and a strong-featured face. She was currently wearing jeans and a rainbow T-shirt. She was a few years younger than Amber would have been, maybe seventeen or eighteen.

“You’re the FBI agents?” she said.

“I’m an agent,” Maya said. “Detective Spinelli here is on loan to the FBI as a consultant. You’re…”

“Erika. Amber’s sister. Mom said to show you in.”

She waved them inside, and Marco’s first impression was of an apartment that had been lived in for a *long* time. There were shelves set around the walls with small ornaments and more books than they could really hold, so that they spilled over into piles. There was a jumble of coats set on hooks near the door. There were pictures on the walls that had been there so long it seemed that the walls had faded around them.

Marco followed Erika and Maya through into a living room where a man and a woman sat together on a dark fabric sofa. Erika went to sit between them. Marco guessed that these must be Amber’s parents. They were both around fifty.

The woman was tall, with slightly graying dark hair cut shoulder length, and the same strong features as her daughter. She was wearing a dark dress with a lighter cardigan thrown over it. Marco couldn’t help noticing that her nails looked as though she'd been biting them, perhaps in some kind of nervous habit since she'd heard that they were coming.

The man was a little shorter, with curly, unkempt dark hair and glasses that helped to soften an otherwise square face. He was wearing a light shirt and dark slacks, and pinched the bridge of his nose as Marco came in, as if the tension of their arrival was starting to bring on a headache.

"Sit down, sit down," the woman said, obviously trying to be friendly. Even so, her nerves came through. "I'm Suzi, this is my husband, Art."

"A pleasure to meet you," Maya said, taking a seat. "I wish it could be under better circumstances. I'm Agent Gray, with the FBI's cold case unit. This is Detective Spinelli, who is working with me as a consultant."

Marco nodded his hello, but hung back by the door, observing. He knew by now to let Maya take the lead in these interviews. Often, she saw things or picked up on things that he didn't. Besides, this was her case.

"You want to talk to us about Amber?" Art said. "Does that mean that you've found whoever… did that to her?"

Maya shook her head, and Marco heard her tone soften. "Not yet. I'm here because the FBI is taking a look at her case."

"The FBI did that before," Erika said, from her spot on the sofa. "They came and asked questions, then went away because it 'didn't fit their profile.'"

She managed to convey exactly how much disdain she felt for that.

"They were investigating one specific serial killer," Maya said. "I'm here to investigate your sister's death, no matter where that investigation leads."

"And why is the FBI doing that?" Art Kaley asked.

"There's a broader investigation going on," Maya said, "the details of which I can't share right now. Rest assured, though, that I have *every* incentive to find Amber's killer."

Marco could hear the determination in those words. He had no doubt that Maya was going to find the killer, no matter what it took.

"What I need from you," Maya went on, "is to know more about Amber. I need to know who she was, what she did, what she was like."

Suzi Kaley answered that, with a catch in her voice. "Amber was a delight. She was a nurse, dedicated to helping people. Her friends loved her. Her colleagues loved her. When she… passed, we got so many messages of condolence from the people who knew her."

"I'm going to be a nurse too," Erika said, with a note of determination. "Like Amber was. I didn't know what I was going to do with my life, but then it was the obvious thing to do."

Marco found himself wondering how Amber's death had affected her sister. It sounded as though she was trying to fill a gap in her life in the shape of her sister, and found himself wondering if it was what she really wanted, or just what she thought she ought to do to make some kind of meaning of it all. He'd seen the aftershocks of murder so many times now, and it never ceased to have a profound impact on the lives of people around the ones who were killed.

"Did she live alone?" Maya asked. "No roommates, partners?"

"She said she needed her space," Art said. He sounded almost guilty as he said that. "If she hadn't moved out, if she'd still been here with us, I might have… I could have protected her."

Suzi Kaley put a hand on her husband's arm. "No one could have. She would still have gone jogging if she lived here."

Now, Marco knew, came the difficult part of this. Asking about Amber's life was one thing, but he knew as well as Maya what they really needed to know.

"Did anyone dislike Amber?" he asked. "Was anyone arguing with her at the time of her death? Did she have any enemies?"

He heard Amber's mother laugh at that. "They asked us that question right after Amber died, but who has enemies? Not our daughter. People loved her. She had so many friends."

"But it had to be someone close to her, right?" Art said. "We discussed this, Suzi. Someone targeted her. It wasn't just random. It can't have been. Someone knew where she would be. That means someone close to her killed her."

Marco guessed that in the time since Amber's death, they'd had plenty of time to think about that likelihood. Probably, they'd thought of little else, looking at each of their daughter's friends and trying to work out which of them might have taken Amber from them. He could only imagine how hard that might have been for them.

"Did she have any money troubles?" Maya asked. "Any trouble at work? Any recent breakups?"

"Nothing like that," Art Kaley said.

Even as he said it, though, Marco could see that Erika was looking uncomfortable. Marco's guess was that she didn't quite agree with her father, but wasn't happy with openly contradicting him in front of the FBI.

Maya obviously caught that look as well. Of course she did. Maya didn't miss things like that. It was just one of the many impressive things about her.

"What is it, Erika?" she asked, in a surprisingly gentle tone given how much she must have been feeling the urgency of the situation. "Have you thought of something that we need to know about?"

"It's probably nothing," Erika said, but she looked away while she said it. She didn't believe that, even if it was what she thought she ought to say. A part of Marco wanted to press her for more, but he could see Maya hanging back, waiting for the young woman to offer up the information of her own accord. "I mean, the police looked at it at the time."

"But you obviously still think that there's something we need to know," Marco suggested. Why else would the young woman bring it up like this? Whatever it was, however slim a lead, it was a starting point.

Erika hesitated for another couple of seconds before she spoke. "Well… like I said, I'm planning to become a nurse like Amber. And… I heard things. About how she wasn't having such a good time at work before she died. About how things were pretty tough for her there. I don't really have any details, though."

"It's something, at least," Maya said.

"But like I said, the police looked at it all. They asked questions at her work. They didn't find anything."

"They aren't us," Maya assured the young woman. "Whatever was going on at the hospital, we'll find it."

Marco already knew that was where they would be heading next. When Amber seemed to have no obvious enemies, even a small hint like that was something they had to chase down.

They would be heading to the hospital next, and Marco could only hope that they found answers there that the police hadn't been able to.

CHAPTER EIGHT

Maya looked up at the university hospital with a sudden sense of how hard it might be to find out everything about Amber Kaley there. The building towered over her, square, blocky, and brick built. Hundreds of people probably worked there, and it would see many thousands of patients a year. Then there were the students passing through, learning their jobs.

As a nurse, Amber would have come into contact with many of them, which meant a potentially huge pool of suspects. The idea of trying to go through all of them in less than two days seemed nearly impossible, and Maya found herself just standing there, staring.

"Breathe, Maya," Marco told her. "You've got this."

It was nice to hear, but it didn't exactly tell her how to start going about this. The more she found herself looking up at the building, though, the more Maya found herself thinking of the FBI headquarters where she worked.

If she needed to find out about herself there, it wouldn't be a matter of asking everyone in the building. It would be about focusing in closer and closer, until she found the few people there who knew her.

"Are you ready to go in?" Marco asked her. Maya was impressed by how well he knew her by now, able to spot exactly the moment when she was ready to head inside.

She stepped into the hospital, into the near chaos of a busy reception area. There were patients waiting in something closer to a huddle rather than a queue in front of the reception desk, some of them pushing to move forward with a vigor that made Maya wonder just how unwell they actually were.

Maya took out her ID, holding it in front of her as she moved through the small crowd like a kind of shield. It meant that she could push through without people pushing her back, people starting to react, then stepping back as they saw her ID.

If there had been more time, she wouldn't have pushed quite so much. She might have waited until she finally reached the space in front of the reception desk. The receptionist was a harassed-looking woman in her forties, who looked over horn-rimmed glasses at Maya, staring at her ID in a way that didn't seem particularly impressed.

"I'm Agent Gray, with the FBI. I need to talk to someone about Amber Kaley, a former nurse here."

"Do you have an appointment?" the receptionist asked.

"No," Maya replied. The simple fact was that there hadn't been enough time. Waiting around for appointments would eat up hours that she simply didn't have. "I just need to talk to people who worked on the same unit as her, or who might have known her. Can you check with someone, please?"

"Well, I suppose I could, but the patients—"

"This is a murder inquiry," Maya pointed out. "If you could just point me to where I need to go and who I need to talk to, you can get back to dealing with everything here."

She heard the receptionist sigh, and then the woman started to tap away at the computer in front of her.

"Amber Kaley? The nurse who was killed?"

It felt like Maya's turn to sigh in frustration. Hadn't the woman been listening to her?

"Yes, that's right."

"She used to work on the fifth floor, in the cardiac unit."

"Will there be people up there who might remember her?" Maya asked.

"Possibly, but—"

"Then that's where I need to go," Maya put in, before the other woman could raise any objections. "Thank you for your help."

She stepped away and let the press of the crowd take over before the receptionist could object.

"We're just pushing past the receptionist?" Marco asked, as the two of them headed for the elevator. He sounded slightly concerned, as if he was worried that Maya was starting to go too far.

She knew that she had in the past, but railroading one receptionist to avoid wading through acres of red tape didn't feel even close to the same.

"We don't have any time," Maya said. "All I want to do is try to find someone who knew Amber."

They headed up to the fifth floor, and the cardiac unit there. Maya found herself looking at the files Samit had sent over. There were some interviews there with the staff, and Maya found herself skimming them, trying to get a sense of what the Philadelphia police had already asked.

"The police at the time seemed to ask a lot about Amber's patients," Maya said, as she read.

"They were working on the theory that one of them was upset enough with her to kill her?" Marco asked. He was possibly thinking of their previous case, where they'd caught the killer just as he'd been attempting to murder a nurse for almost exactly that reason.

Maya could understand why it might be plausible. People could react strongly in relation to their medical conditions, particularly if they didn't get the treatment they thought they required. Yet the police had found nothing with that line of questioning.

The elevator doors slid open, and Maya headed into the cardiac unit. There was another receptionist there, and this one looked considerably less harassed as she went about her work than the one downstairs. She was in her twenties, with short dark hair, smartly dressed in a skirt, blouse, and jacket, and she wore a gold pendant.

"Can I help you?" she asked.

Maya presented her ID.

"I don't have an appointment, but I was hoping I could ask some questions about Amber Kaley, a nurse who used to work here, who was killed about a year ago."

"You want to talk about Amber?" the receptionist replied, and her professional mask slipped a little. She looked both surprised and suddenly hurt. Maya could guess why.

"You knew Amber, then?"

She saw the receptionist nod. "I've worked here for a couple of years now. I know people move on from this kind of job pretty quickly, but I've always loved working in a hospital, being a part of the work we do here. Amber… Amber was my friend."

Maya looked over to Marco. It seemed that they'd found someone who might be able to tell them about the victim. At the very least, she would be able to tell them who else they needed to talk to.

"What's your name?" Maya asked her, leaning on the reception desk.

"I'm Daisy."

"And you knew Amber well?"

Daisy nodded. "The two of us and a couple of the other nurses would go out for drinks sometimes after work. Although we always had to persuade her to skip her run for the evening if we wanted to do that."

"She was an avid runner, then?" Marco asked from the side.

They'd both heard Samit talking about Amber's running data when it came to the murder scene, but Maya had to admit that it would be helpful to know more about exactly how seriously she'd taken it all.

"She took it super seriously," Daisy replied. "I tried going running with her a couple of times, but I couldn't even start to keep up."

So Amber might well have been able to get away from her killer if she'd seen them coming. Was that another reason they'd ambushed her where they had? To give her no chance to try to run to safety?

"And was she well liked here?" Maya asked.

"What? Yes, of course," Daisy replied, as if the thought that things could be any other way simply didn't make sense to her. "Everybody here loved her. She was popular, she was good at her job, the patients adored her—"

"Did anyone here seem to like her *too* much?" Marco put in. It was a good thought. Obsession could be just as big a driver toward murder as hatred, particularly if that obsession wasn't reciprocated.

Daisy looked slightly puzzled by that. "What do you mean?"

Maya tried to think of the best way to put it. "Did Amber ever complain that anyone was being creepy toward her? Harassing her, maybe? Sending her gifts she didn't want or trying to call her?"

The receptionist shook her head. "No, nothing like that. If there had been, I would have told the police right after she was… right after she died."

Maya could see the upset on the young woman's face, and apparently so could someone else.

"Is everything all right, Daisy?"

Maya turned to see a tall man in pale blue surgical scrubs. He was thin-faced and slightly hollow-eyed in a way that made him look as if he'd been working far too many hours in one shift.

"Who are you," he asked, "and why are you upsetting the receptionist for my unit?"

"Agent Gray, FBI," Maya said, holding out her ID. "That's Detective Spinelli, who's consulting with me. We're reinvestigating the death of Amber Kaley. When you say 'your unit'…"

"I am Dr. Graham Henrik, the head of the cardiac surgery department here," the doctor said. "If you want to talk about my staff, then you should really talk to me."

"We'd be happy to do so," Maya said. She took in the slight stains on his scrubs and the sense of tiredness around his eyes. "I take it that you're coming out of surgery, rather than going into it?"

She saw Dr. Henrik nod. "A successful coarctation repair on a six-week-old child. Five hours, so I hope you'll understand if I want to make this brief."

"That's fine." There was nothing Maya wanted more. She and Marco were already eating into their first day. "But I *would* like to ask you a couple of questions about Amber, if that's all right?"

"Yes, of course." He waved the two of them over to a couple of chairs in the unit's waiting area, where they sat opposite him. "What do you need to know?"

"I take it that you worked with her?" Maya said.

He nodded. "Nurse Kaley was very good at her job, and liked by all the patients."

That was almost exactly what the receptionist had told her, and what was in the police report as well. Taken together, it meant that Maya could be pretty sure that there were no obvious suspects among Amber's patients.

"What about her colleagues?" Maya asked. "Did she ever have any trouble with any of the other people who worked here?"

"Not that I know of. Oh, I'm sure there would have been the usual minor disagreements and so on, but nothing major."

That was frustrating, in a way, with the lack of anything obvious to go on, but then, if anything had been obvious, Maya was sure that Detective Tanner would have found an answer in the days after Amber's death. Maya needed to find a way to dig deeper.

"Did anyone behave strangely around the time of Amber's death?" she asked. "It doesn't matter if it was obviously about her. Anything at all might help."

Dr. Henrik started to shake his head, but then stopped himself. "Well, I suppose there was the fact that Dr. Fulbright quit a week or two afterwards."

"Who is Dr. Fulbright?" Marco asked, looking on with a sudden intensity that matched what Maya felt right then.

“He was one of our residents on this unit. Very promising. We were even talking about him getting a promotion.”

“But he quit? Right after Amber’s death?” Maya asked.

“Yes. Of course, he might just have been affected by the tragedy of it. I know we all were.”

Perhaps that was true. Perhaps this was a man who had just decided that he couldn’t work in the hospital after one of his colleagues had been murdered. Yet Maya’s instincts told her that there was the potential for there to be more. At the very least, quitting because of the murder suggested some kind of closer relationship than the rest of the staff there had with Amber.

It might also suggest much more. It *might* be a guilty man wanting to put some distance between himself and the site of an investigation.

Either way, Maya needed to know a lot more about this Dr. Fulbright.

CHAPTER NINE

As Maya left the hospital, there was one lead that she wanted to chase down right away: Dr. Fulbright. His leaving so soon after Amber's death might mean nothing, but far more of her felt that there was something strange about the timing, something that she wanted to investigate further.

Heading back to Marco's car, she got out her laptop and logged into the FBI's systems. It felt strange to be doing this kind of thing in a car rather than having a borrowed office somewhere in a local police department, but Maya was also used to doing work on the move, and maybe this would prove quicker than having to go back and forth to some central base.

"You're checking out the doctor who left?" Marco asked.

Maya nodded. "It just seems odd that he quit when he did. Maybe it's a coincidence, but…"

"But it's far more likely that there's some kind of connection to the death," Marco finished for her. "It might just be that he couldn't stand being there after one of his colleagues had died."

Maya understood that, but it wasn't enough to make her back away on this. "Even that suggests some kind of connection. Other people there didn't quit, even when they were Amber's friend, like Daisy was. So does that mean that Dr. Fulbright had some kind of closer connection that no one knew about?"

"You're thinking he was seeing her?" Marco asked.

Maya shrugged. "I don't know what to think yet."

She typed in Dr. Fulbright's name on the computer, doing the basics by checking if he had a criminal record, if there were any FBI flags attached to his name. Nothing came up. From what she could see from the case files, he hadn't even come under scrutiny in the police investigations.

She got his DMV details, though, and the details of his professional registration. It meant that she had an address for him in Philadelphia, and a first name: Grant.

She called Samit.

"Hi, Samit, I need access to whatever's left of Amber Kaley's social media accounts. I want to look at her call records and her messages. Can you do that for me?"

"We're in luck," Samit said. "The original investigation on our side seems to have trawled through her social media. I'll send it over to you."

A few seconds later, Maya's computer pinged as the information came through. She opened up a browser, ready to look through it all, trying to find some kind of connection between Amber and Dr. Fulbright.

"I'll google the doctor," Marco said. "See if there's anything about him out there that might be relevant."

"Thanks," Maya said. It was good to have another set of eyes on this that she could trust. She knew that if there was something out there to be found, Marco would find it.

That left her with the social media, and Maya started to trawl through it, looking for any sign of Dr. Fulbright. In particular, she found herself hoping that she would find either some sign of conflict between him and Amber Kaley or some sign of romance between the two of them.

Either of them could have proved to be a motive for murder.

There were a few signs of him in Amber's feed, but only as many as Maya might have expected from the kind of casual acquaintance or work colleague that… well, that he was.

He didn't even seem to be a follower or a friend on half the platforms there. There just didn't seem to be that much of a connection between the two of them, and that was kind of disappointing. Maya had been expecting… well, more.

Even when she started to go through Amber's messages, there was nothing. There were a couple of casual messages, which seemed to be about work, a couple of "Hey, how are things going" messages, and nothing beyond that. Certainly nothing that might count as an indication of a potential murderer.

"We might be looking at the wrong guy," Marco said. "There's nothing out there that suggests any kind of problem with this guy. There are a few links to the private practice that he works in these days, a couple of links to his current social media, and a reference to a paper that he wrote on improving the functioning of bicuspid aortic valves, but that's it."

Maya had been half hoping that there might be a news article talking about complaints about the doctor in some other hospital, or about ways he'd harassed staff in some other location. That might have pointed to him as a real suspect, but as it was, it looked as if they'd struck out.

Even so, there was something about Dr. Fulbright's sudden exit that made her want to find a way to keep digging.

Maya found herself calling Samit again, putting him on speaker so that Marco could hear.

"Agent Gray, did you find something?"

"No," Maya said. "That's the problem. There doesn't seem to be any real link here between Amber Kaley and Dr. Fulbright. I feel so sure that there should be something, but if I can't actually find it, then I can't waste any more time on this."

"Would the hospital have a private messaging system?" Samit asked.

Maya frowned at the thought of that. "Is that likely?"

"A lot do. They want to be able to communicate among themselves, but a commercial social network isn't appropriate when there might be patient details involved. Plenty of them use the same providers."

Maya knew in that moment that if there was such a system, she needed to get a look at it.

"Is there any way of telling if they *do* have a system like that?"

"This is the university hospital, right? OK… yes, it looks like they're using one of the major providers for it."

Maya looked over to Marco before she said the next part. "We need to look at that message board. If Dr. Fulbright had any real contact with Amber, it was there."

Marco looked a little troubled by that. "You know the hospital won't just let you into its messaging system without a warrant, not if there's a risk of patient details being on there."

He had a point. If Maya went back into the hospital to ask for permission, they would undoubtedly tell her no. They would *have* to tell her no, regardless of the fact that she was looking into a murder. None of the doctors would risk their medical licenses by doing anything else.

"It's going to take too long to get a warrant," Maya said. "Even if we had probable cause, and I'm pretty sure we don't, it would take hours at least, possibly until tomorrow. We'd never get access to the messages in time."

They only had today and tomorrow. If they spent all their remaining time on this hunch, and nothing came of it, there wouldn't be any time in which to look anywhere else. A woman would die. At the same time, though, if they *didn't* get access to those messages, and it turned out that Dr. Fulbright was the killer, then they had no way of proving anything.

"I can get you in," Samit said.

"Samit, without a warrant, the hospital won't allow us access."

"OK, so it won't exactly be legit, but I can… sorry, I shouldn't be talking like this."

Maya knew that she had to ask the next question. "Samit, are you saying that you can hack into the message system used by this provider?"

"Yes. There's an exploit in the system they're using that means that I can spoof an ID, and—"

"And you can give us access," Marco said. "Only problem is, isn't that illegal?"

"Um…" Samit didn't answer for a second or two.

"And we wouldn't be able to use any evidence from it in court," Marco pointed out.

Which would make it hard to get a conviction. At the same time, though, it was the only way that they were likely to get to see those messages, the only way that they were likely to know whether there was actually any kind of conflict between Dr. Fulbright and Amber Kaley.

If they found something, Maya would *find* a way to get a warrant and make the whole thing legal. In any case, when it came down to it, she didn't need to convince a court; she just needed to show the Moonlight Killer that she had found the murderer. Right then, that was the thing that might save her sister's life. That took priority over everything.

"I know that it's not the kind of thing I'm supposed to suggest," Samit said. "But I know what's at stake as well as the two of you do. If there really isn't any time for a warrant…"

"Do it," Maya said, before she could change her mind. Some situations didn't allow enough time to do everything by the book.

"All right," Samit said. "Give me a minute or two."

Maya looked over to Marco, who gave her a level look.

"Are you sure this is the right thing to do?" he asked.

"I don't think we have many other choices. Don't worry, this is my decision. If there's any fallout from this, I'll make sure it only comes down on me."

"That's what I'm worried about," Marco said. "I'm worried that you'll do absolutely anything you need to in order to save your sister, regardless of how deep down the rabbit hole it takes you."

"Wouldn't you?" Maya said, with a challenging look.

Marco didn't get a chance to answer, though, because Samit chose that moment to speak again.

"OK, we're in. You should have access via your laptop now."

In its way, it was slightly worrying, the ease with which Samit had managed to get access. It suggested to Maya that nothing was truly secure, and only served to remind her that the Moonlight Killer was probably listening in to every call she made, including this one.

Maya started to look through the messages on the internal service, and now it was easy to find ones between Amber and Dr. Fulbright.

The first ones seemed to suggest that he had some kind of thing for her.

Hey, Amber. Just wondering if you were doing anything this Friday night? Thought we could get dinner.

Her reply was short and to the point.

Sorry, but I'm already doing something on Friday. See you at work on Monday.

Maybe some guys would have gotten the message there, but the next communication between the two of them made it clear that Dr. Fulbright hadn't even come close to understanding that Amber wanted him to back off.

I really think you looked great yesterday. I find myself thinking about you all the time. I really wish you'd just come out for a drink with me. I know you'd enjoy it.

I'm sorry, Grant, but I'm just not interested. Please stop asking me. Your comments at work aren't appropriate, either.

The messages didn't seem to slow down, though. They continued with the same tone, the same attempts to get Amber to see him, as if Dr. Fulbright just didn't see the attempts to reject him.

You do know that you have lovely eyes, right? I stand in surgery, and I can't see the rest of your face because of your mask, but your eyes are amazing.

Then, suddenly, there was a shift in tone.

You bitch. I've made so much effort with you, and you've just thrown it back in my face. I hope you die!

You spent so long stringing me along. Women like you are all the same. One of these days, you'll get what's coming to you.

Maya looked at the dates for those messages, and a sense of excitement filled her as she did so. Those last couple of messages had been sent just a week before Amber Kaley died.

They had to talk to Dr. Grant Fulbright, right now.

CHAPTER TEN

Megan wasn't sure how long she and the others had been down here now, in the bunker that formed their prison, and she found that not knowing ate at her.

She was in a position where she had almost no power over her life. She ate and slept when her kidnapper told her to, was free to walk around or locked in a cage on his whim. She didn't even have the power to keep herself safe here. *That* came down to what was happening in the outside world.

Megan had the bruises to prove that, inflicted because someone at the FBI had done the wrong thing.

Not her sister, though. Megan had to trust, *did* trust, that Maya was doing everything she could to get them out of there. She'd gotten several of them out of there already. Megan had to believe that sooner or later, it would be her turn.

For now, she was out of her cage. The kidnapper had finally let her and the others loose, so that the remaining seven of them got to walk around the tunnels that he'd either built or found.

Megan had seen the fury in his eyes earlier, after Haley had killed herself. They were the only part of him that any of them got to see, normally, and for Megan, that was a good thing. A man who just intended to kill them all wouldn't be so cautious about avoiding being seen. It wouldn't make any difference to him.

At the same time, there was a coldness in his eyes that terrified Megan. That coldness said that he didn't care, didn't see them as anything even human, for all that he talked about them all like they were favored pets. Even when he'd been hurting her, ignoring Megan's screams of pain, there had been that dead look, like it was all just some kind of chore to him.

Megan put that out of her mind, making her way around the tunnels of the bunker. She and the others were allowed to move as they pleased when they weren't locked in their cages for lights out. The gray, featureless walls seemed identical at first, but Megan had walked the small confines of the place so many times now that she knew every scuff, every nut and bolt, by heart.

Finding the details helped her stay sane down there, but there was another part to it for Megan: every detail she remembered was one she would be able to tell Maya once she got out of here, or pass on to one of the others when *they* were released.

And they *would* be released. Maya would solve any case their captor put in front of her. Megan was sure of it. Her sister wouldn't fail.

The thought of what might happen if Maya ever did fail was one that filled Megan with terror. She'd looked into the eyes of the man who held them. She had no doubt at all that he would kill them, one by one, if Maya failed. Would Megan be the first, to hurt her more if she failed, or would he save her until last, not wanting to let go of that piece of leverage over her sister?

Neither one was a comforting thought, and to push it from her mind, Megan focused her attention on the other women there.

All of them wore identical gray jumpsuits. All of them were disheveled after so long in captivity, gaunt with the stress of it, and with how erratically their captor fed them. If the bunker said just how carefully he'd planned all of this, other aspects of his behavior suggested that he hadn't considered everything that might come with holding twelve women hostage.

Megan had another flash of fear then, this one stronger. What if he decided that it was too much trouble for whatever plan he was working through? What if he decided that he couldn't take holding the rest of them any longer? Would he just let them go if there wasn't any reason to? If her sister hadn't solved all the crimes he set for her to unpick?

Megan doubted, somehow, that he would just open up their cages and tell them all to run free.

She moved around the others. They were quiet, today. They'd seen two deaths in less than two weeks, first with Carmel, and then Haley. Megan could see the fear on their faces that they might be next.

Megan knew their names by now: Melissa, Saoirse, Francine, Imogen, Lucy. And, of course, Tori, the kidnapper's latest victim.

"We have to stay strong," Megan said, moving to Melissa and putting a hand on her shoulder. She was short and slender, with curly blonde hair and a tendency to cry in the night when she thought no one could hear. Megan had learned that she'd just left a bad relationship when she was snatched.

"That's easy for you to say," Melissa replied. "You know he won't kill *you* next."

"He's not going to kill you," Megan assured her, putting a hand over hers. "My sister is going to solve whatever case he's given her, and one of us will be released."

She went to Saoirse, who was red-haired and green-eyed, fine boned and with a faint Irish accent even though she'd apparently never been to Ireland. She'd been planning to move there when she'd been taken.

"Are you doing OK?" Megan asked.

"What do you think, after what happened to the others?"

"He wants us alive, though," Megan said. "I know it's hard, but he obviously wants that. Just look at how angry he was because of what happened to Haley."

It was hard, trying to reassure the others when she didn't really know anything about what was going on. Megan tried to pick up every scrap of information she could, but she was all too aware that she didn't have her sister's powers of observation or deduction.

Still, she'd worked some things out. She'd spotted the physical similarities between herself and everyone else here, all slender and fine boned, almost fragile looking. She'd worked out something else too: that every woman there seemed to have been on the verge of some new stage in her life when the kidnapper had taken her.

For Megan, it hadn't been that she'd been traveling around the country, trying to find herself. No, it had been the part where she'd decided to *stop* traveling, to come back and re-enroll in school, to get her life on track the way her sister had.

She'd been having one last night out when she'd been taken, grabbed and hooded with such speed that it was obvious it had been planned well before. Which meant that someone had been watching her before that point. Someone had followed her and gathered information. Probably the kidnapper, but maybe someone working for him.

The problem was that Megan couldn't remember any of that surveillance. She couldn't remember a single moment that had been out of place. The only thing she'd been able to remember from the moment of her kidnapping was something she'd already passed on to her sister: the details of the kidnapper's tattoo.

At least, she hoped she had. She'd sent the information out with one of the women who'd been released, but the very nature of their incarceration meant that Megan had no way of knowing if she had reached Maya, or if she had remembered the information once she had.

Megan had to hope, though, and that meant that she needed more. She needed every scrap that she could find, in the hope that something would be the crucial piece that would let her sister find the kidnapper.

The best chance to get new information was to talk to the kidnapper's newest victim. Megan had spoken to the others. They hadn't been able to give her anything that she could pass on to Megan. Now, she needed to hope that Tori had seen more than any of them had.

Megan had to be careful how she did this, though. She knew the kidnapper was watching, probably closer than ever now that both Carmel and Haley had tried to escape him in their own ways.

It was a part of why she went to the others before she made her way over to Tori, although the other part of it was that she truly wanted to make sure that she did all she could to keep them from despairing.

Finally, Megan went over to the spot where Tori sat huddled with her back against one scratched and dirt-streaked patch of wall in the main chamber of the bunker, the one where the kidnapper kept a single chair, like the throne of some king. This was the chamber he summoned them to when he wanted to talk to them.

Tori was slender, tanned, and dark haired, with large dark eyes that seemed red with the amount she must have been crying. Her arms were wrapped around herself, as if she might protect herself that way.

Megan crouched next to Tori, not saying anything for the first few moments. Slowly, carefully, she reached out a hand for Tori's arm.

The other woman flinched, as if afraid of that touch.

"I'm not going to hurt you," Megan told her. "I know you're terrified right now. I know what you saw was too much."

"She… she just killed herself, right there, in front of all of us."

Megan wished she could tell the young woman that it was the worst thing that she would see there, or the worst thing that she would experience. Yet so far, there had been beatings, deaths, a woman had been made to cut off her own finger… Megan was sure that it wasn't done. Not even close.

"I know," Megan said. "I knew Haley, at least a little. Getting to know one another is all we have, down here."

Tori shrugged at that, not venturing an answer just yet.

"Can you tell me anything about yourself?" Megan said.

"Why?" The word was quiet, and also closed off.

"Because it might make you feel better if you don't feel that you're alone here," Megan said.

"I… I'm an artist. Or I was going to be, before…" Tori gestured to the gray walls of the bunker around them.

"You still will be," Megan reassured her.

"You don't know that."

Tori was silent for several seconds.

"No," Megan said. "You're right. I don't know for sure. I can't guarantee that either of us will be safe, but my sister is doing everything she can to get us out of here. And I want to help her."

"How?" Tori asked.

"It might help if you tell me about how you were taken," Megan suggested. "Anything you can remember, anything about the man who took you, might help."

Tori didn't answer, though. "I… I can't."

"I know you're afraid," Megan said. "I know you think that if you say anything, it will make things worse, but it won't. How could things get worse than this? But it might help."

"How?" Tori asked.

"Because any information you have, I will try to get out to my sister with whoever gets released," Megan replied. There was no point in holding it back, not when she would have to tell all the others there whatever she found out, so that whoever *he* chose would be able to carry the information back to Maya.

Tori sat there for several seconds, obviously thinking.

"There was one thing. When he took me, it was like he was favoring his left leg. Like he had some kind of old injury there."

"You're sure?" Megan asked.

"I'm not sure about anything right now." Tori went quiet after that.

She was obviously too scared, or didn't trust Megan enough, to keep going.

Megan knew she ought to back off, but she also knew that she couldn't. She had to keep trying. She didn't even know if her attempts to get information out to Maya were succeeding, but she had to hope. She had to hope that Maya was getting the information, and that it was helping her in at least some small way.

She had to keep trying with Tori, and in the meantime, she just had to hope that Maya was getting closer to all of them.

CHAPTER ELEVEN

Maya spotted Dr. Fulbright's name on a plaque by the door of the Wellbeing Medical Practice. It was at the bottom, after four others, but it was there. This, apparently, was what he'd left the hospital to do.

The practice itself was in an older building that had been renovated to the point where there almost wasn't anything of the original structure left. The exterior façade looked as if it had been there a hundred years, but the interior was all polished metal and chic grays. Even the furniture in the waiting area was modern and ergonomic, rather than the standard ranks of plastic chairs.

There were a couple of people waiting, but the room was nowhere near as packed as the ones at the university hospital had been. Maya guessed that the people who came here weren't paying to be kept waiting.

A reception desk sat toward the front, next to a corridor that presumably led to the various doctors' offices, in an expensive-looking mix of walnut and teak. A young man sat behind it, looking as professional as if he were managing a bank rather than staffing the reception for a private medical practice. He was wearing a dark suit and had slicked back black hair. His smile was almost professionally dazzling as he greeted them.

"Welcome to the Wellbeing Medical Practice. I'm Calvin. How may I help you today?"

"I'd like to see Dr. Fulbright, please," Maya said.

"Do you have an appointment?"

Maya put her ID down on the counter so the receptionist would be able to see it without it being too obvious. She had a feeling that this was the kind of place that valued discretion, and for the moment at least, she was willing to go along with it. She suspected that the polite approach was likely to get her far more cooperation than anything more obvious.

"No, but I hope that he'll have time to speak to me and my colleague. It's urgent."

There was a brief crack in the professional façade of the receptionist, and Maya saw the worry there. She guessed that he wasn't used to anything more challenging than an unhappy patient or a pushy rep from a pharmaceutical company.

"Can you ask Dr. Fulbright to come out to speak to us please, Calvin?" Marco asked, moving to stand beside Maya at the desk, keeping up the pressure. He obviously knew as well as Maya did that they didn't have enough time for a lengthy delay. If they had to sit in the waiting room while Dr. Fulbright took his time about coming out to see them, then they were wasting time that they needed to use to progress in this case.

"I… I'll call him." Calvin picked up a phone and punched in a number to dial internally.

At the same time, though, the wait would be worth it if Dr. Fulbright proved to be the killer. If Maya and Marco had found the killer on their first day here, then they still had time in which to ensure that there was a watertight case against him afterwards.

"Dr. Fulbright, there are some people here to see you. They say it's urgent. Yes, I understand that."

They would have to put time into getting more proof even if their conversation with Dr. Fulbright raised more suspicions. He wasn't just going to come out and admit that he was the killer. In that moment, Maya found herself starting to worry more about the way they'd gotten here, with Samit's hack on the hospital's systems. What if Dr. Fulbright *did* prove to be the killer? They would have to spend time then trying to find evidence to back that up that hadn't come from an illegal source.

Calvin lowered his voice. "They're from the FBI."

Maya realized then that the need to act to save her sister had pushed her once more into doing something she would never have done just a few weeks ago, yet even now, she couldn't truly regret it. She hadn't been given enough time to do things any other way.

Maybe that was a part of what the Moonlight Killer was doing with all of this. Obviously he had his own agenda when it came to the investigations, but maybe some small part of it was to see exactly how far Maya would go in order to protect the women whose lives the serial killer was currently threatening.

That thought was an uncomfortable one. Was all of this changing her in ways that she wouldn't like when it came to the end? When she finally got Megan back, would her own sister even recognize who she was anymore? Would she finally catch the Moonlight Killer, only for him to smile over at her and tell Maya that she had become everything he'd hoped she would?

"Dr. Fulbright will be right out," Calvin said. He gestured to the waiting area. "If you'd like to take a seat?"

Actually, what Maya *wanted* to do was to go through the offices to make sure that Dr. Fulbright wasn't using this chance to make a run for it. The receptionist's call might bring him out to them, but if he really was the murderer, it might also give him enough warning to try to make his escape.

Yet she also knew that she couldn't just barge through the medical practice without a warrant, or at least not without some indication that the doctor was actually trying to leave. A part of her wanted to do it anyway, but after everything she'd just thought, Maya couldn't bring herself to do it. She forced herself to sit down, telling herself that Dr. Fulbright would be out to see them soon enough.

And if he didn't come out to them in five minutes, *then* Maya would make her way through the practice to find him, probably with her gun drawn.

"Are you OK?" Marco asked as they waited.

"I just hate waiting." Maya's fingers drummed out the passing seconds. She should be using this time to look at other possible leads. She should be doing something.

"Dr. Fulbright is our best lead at the moment, and Samit is still working other angles back at headquarters," Marco pointed out. He obviously knew exactly what Maya was feeling. "If you're trying to run in every direction at once, you won't get answers in any of them."

Maya knew that was true, but it didn't make it any easier to wait. It seemed like forever before a man in his thirties came out from the corridor leading to the offices. He was maybe an inch or so taller than Maya's five-ten, with short cropped blond hair and blue eyes. He wore dark slacks and a pale pink shirt with the sleeves rolled up to the elbows. A stethoscope sat around his neck.

He didn't look happy as he went over to the receptionist.

"OK, Calvin, where are these people?"

Maya guessed that this was the man they'd come to see, so she stood up, moving over to the reception desk again. She had her ID ready.

"I'm Agent Gray with the FBI. This is Detective Spinelli, who is consulting with me."

Marco held out his own taskforce ID for the doctor to look at.

If anything, that only made him look less happy.

"Keep your voices down! We pride ourselves on being a *discreet* medical practice for a *select* clientele. Do you know that you've just pulled me out of a consultation about a potential arterial stenosis with a *very* important figure?"

Maya could hear the anger there. Was that the anger of someone who was just upset at being called away from his job, or was it the anger of a man trying to avoid answering questions?

"So discreet that you're talking about a possible diagnosis here in the waiting area?" Marco said.

Dr. Fulbright huffed and turned as if he might leave and go back to his consultation. Maya said the only thing she could think of to stop him.

"Amber Kaley."

He stopped as suddenly as if Maya had grabbed him. He turned back to her. "What did you say?"

"I'm looking into the death of Amber Kaley. Now, I can ask you questions here in the waiting room with all your patients listening, or—"

"Calvin," Dr. Fulbright said. "Will you ask Dr. Maddison to take over my consultation? I'm afraid I need to talk to these people."

He gestured for Maya and Marco to follow him.

"This way. We'll talk in the conference room."

They had a conference room? Obviously, this was a *long* way from the kind of set-up Maya had seen at the hospital.

Dr. Fulbright led them to a large room dominated by an oval table made from clear glass. Maya and Marco took seats at one side of it, while Dr. Fulbright went over to a coffee machine in the corner, grabbing a cup. Maya noted that he didn't offer her or Marco any. She guessed that he really wasn't happy about them being here.

"Could you sit down, please, Dr. Fulbright?" she said.

He took a seat opposite the two of them, and now he didn't look angry so much as worried.

"I knew this day would come," he said.

For a brief moment, Maya dared to hope that he actually *might* just confess. Maybe he'd been holding back the guilt of what he'd done, and all it took to unlock it all was Amber's name.

"I knew someone would find the messages I sent to Amber."

Ah, so not a confession just yet, then. Still, it was nice to have the confirmation that he had sent those messages.

"You were very"—Maya struggled to think of a word other than "sleazy"—"persistent in your messages. You harassed her, Dr. Fulbright."

"She never made a complaint," Dr. Fulbright replied, as if that made things better. "And it wasn't as if she was the only one. I sent messages to a lot of nurses."

"Maybe Amber didn't feel that she *could* make a complaint," Marco suggested. "You were a doctor at the hospital, after all."

"Was that why you felt that you could keep hitting on her?" Maya asked. "Because she was just a nurse? How many nurses did you hit on, Dr. Fulbright?"

"A few."

He looked pretty guilty in that moment, and Maya just kept looking at him levelly, not saying anything.

"All right, a lot. But I never did anything with any of them that they didn't want."

Maya was pretty sure that wasn't true. She'd seen the messages from Amber, telling him that she wasn't interested, but he'd kept going anyway.

"I doubt Amber wanted you to threaten to kill her," Maya said. "What happened in those last couple of weeks that made you send those messages, Dr. Fulbright?"

The doctor was silent for several seconds.

"Dr. Fulbright?" Marco said, in a harsher tone.

"She was going to talk to management if I didn't back off, OK? She said she'd had enough."

"And so you killed her," Maya suggested.

"That's not what happened!"

Maya waited, giving him space to tell her his version of it all. She'd already established that he had a temper. Pushing further wouldn't get more out of him.

"I… yes, I was angry," Dr. Fulbright said. He spread his hands. "And it was stupid of me to make those threats. Do you think I haven't lived in fear of someone like you showing up, precisely because of those messages? Why do you think I quit?"

"To get away from the hospital after you killed Amber?" Marco suggested. He obviously wasn't in a mood to give any ground to their suspect.

"I didn't kill her," Dr. Fulbright said. "You have to believe me!"

He sounded insistent, sincere, but Maya needed more than that.

"Why should we believe you, Grant? Why should I believe a single word that you say? Look at it from where we're sitting. We've found a doctor who made threats to the victim just before her death, who left the hospital where she worked immediately afterwards, and who is now saying that he was about to face a complaint. What reason do I have to believe that you weren't the one waiting for Amber on her run after work that night?"

"I wasn't there!" Dr. Fulbright insisted, holding up his hands as if he might fend off the accusation.

"Then where were you?" Marco demanded.

"I was… I was seeing another nurse. Becky Reeves, I think."

"You think?" Maya asked. She gave him a serious look. "You need to be very certain about where you were and who you were with right now, Dr. Fulbright."

"Becky Reeves," the doctor repeated. "It wasn't a long-term thing, but that night… I took her out to dinner, we had a few drinks. We ended up back at her place."

"And she'll confirm this?" Marco said.

"I… I hope so."

Maya had the feeling that the doctor was starting to realize that leaving behind a trail of women who hated him probably wasn't good when he needed something from them like an alibi.

At the same time, it would make any alibi coming from the nurse more believable. She had no reason to lie for a sleazeball like this.

"All right," Maya said. "I'll need her number, the name of the restaurant, and any details you can remember about anyone who might have seen you. We *will* check."

"I… yes, of course."

Maya found herself wishing that this was their guy, but with a growing sense of disappointment, she was starting to realize he wasn't. They would look into his alibi, but she suspected that it would check out.

Which meant they'd struck out. They needed to start again. They needed to find another lead.

They needed to go back to the case files, and hope that the truth was buried in there somewhere.

CHAPTER TWELVE

Maya sat in Marco's car, parked in front of a food stand near the Philadelphia Museum of Arts and its famous steps. It beat driving around trying to find somewhere to stay, or trying to prevail upon the local PD for an office they could use. Maya still didn't want to waste a single second if she could help it. Between the drive there and the time spent looking into the leads from the hospital, they were already into the afternoon of their first day. Time felt as if it were slipping through her fingers like sand, impossible to hold onto.

Maya was staring at the case files Samit had sent over on her computer, reading through the witness statements and the official statements by the cops, trying to find any hint that might point her in a new direction.

When Marco pressed a taco into her hand, Maya barely looked up to acknowledge it. She ate mechanically, continuing to go through the file.

"I called Becky Reeves, the nurse Dr. Fulbright claims is his alibi," Marco said.

Maya did look up then, half hoping that she had refused to confirm the alibi, and that Dr. Fulbright might be back on their list of suspects.

"And?"

"And she confirmed what he said, pretty much. She says he harassed her on social media until she agreed to go out on a date with him. They went for dinner, and he pushed her to go for drinks. He got her pretty drunk, and they ended up having a one-night stand. Apparently not a memory she was too eager to revisit."

"So Dr. Fulbright is every bit as much of a scumbag as we thought, but he can't be our murderer?" Maya said.

She saw Marco nod. "Sorry, but no. We have to find someone else."

That was easier said than done. Maya couldn't find any obvious new information in the file. The so-called witnesses were just the people who had found the body, about ten minutes after the presumed time of death, according to the coroner's report.

Plenty of time for the killer to have gotten away, and in a big park, it was impossible to be sure which of the people there might have had anything to do with Amber's death.

There were witness statements from several. None reported anyone unusual, aside from a couple of homeless guys who had later been found and questioned by the local police, and who didn't seem to have anything to do with the case. They'd just been in the wrong place at the wrong time.

Maya went through the coroner's report next, hoping to find any anomaly in the method of murder or in some other aspect of the report that the local police hadn't picked up on. There was nothing, and Maya was starting to think that Detective Tanner was depressingly good at his job.

"There's nothing here, Marco," Maya said, as she finished the last of the taco. She hadn't even really noticed eating it. At this point, it was just fuel. There was a cup of coffee in front of her, and Maya realized that Marco must have put it there. She'd been so wrapped up in trying to find answers that she hadn't even noticed it.

"There has to be something, and you'll find it, whatever it is," Marco assured her. He was going through the files too, on his phone, apparently working through the police reports in case anything stood out.

"What if there isn't anything?" Maya asked. That was her biggest fear in all of this: that she and Marco could put in as much work as humanly possible over the next couple of days, but there simply wasn't anything there to find.

"I think there has to be something," Marco said. "The Moonlight Killer has always had an idea before of who the real killer must be. That means that there must be some evidence somewhere."

He made it sound as if the Moonlight Killer were Sherlock Holmes, deducing the answers from slender fragments of clues well before Maya could. No, not Sherlock, Maya realized with a start. He'd been the active one in those stories, running around and finding answers regardless of the danger. That was closer to her role in all of this. The Moonlight Killer was more like Mycroft Holmes, the older brother who sat in his club all day rather than running after the evidence.

The only problem with that thought was that, in the stories, Mycroft had been the more brilliant of the two. Maya really hoped that wasn't the case here. She had to be smarter than the Moonlight Killer, had to find a way to be better than him, or her sister was going to die.

"We need to at least believe that there is something to find," Marco said. "It's the only way to have any hope in all of this. And I believe in you, Maya. If anyone can find an answer here, it's you."

Maya hoped so, she really did. At least Marco's pep talk meant that she had the energy to throw herself back into the files again, looking through the coroner's report once more, checking the list of Amber's effects to see if there was anything that stood out there. After all, she'd only just solved a case where the killer had planted pieces of a jigsaw puzzle on the women he killed. Maybe there would be something similar here.

None of it seemed relevant, though. The effects listed Amber's running clothes, a purse that still had money in it, an iPod that she'd been listening to as she ran, her phone, a couple of small gold studs in her ears. Those suggested that this wasn't some kind of mugging gone wrong, but did nothing to tell Maya more about who might have done this.

Maya left the coroner's report and started going through what was left of Amber's social media instead. No one had been through the process of deleting it all yet, and most of it had been archived for use in the investigation, so there was plenty to find. Plenty of photographs of Amber out on the town with her friends from the hospital, and plenty more photographs of her running.

It isn't a good day unless I'm running, ran one of the captions, along with a photograph of her stretching up toward the sun after a run in a crop top and leggings. A small sapphire ring shone against the light at her navel.

Maya kept looking, searching for any photographs that seemed out of the ordinary, or any comments that pointed to a deeper animosity with someone. There was nothing there to find, though. Maya had been through all of the messaging side of it before in her search for anyone at the hospital who might have a problem with Amber. There was nothing new to find now, just because Maya needed something to go on.

She needed a break. One downside of working in the car like this was that it meant that she was squashed up in a not particularly comfortable position, her lower back tightening with the position she was forced into as she tried to balance her laptop and go through all the files.

Maya set it aside for a moment or two. As much as she wanted to keep pushing forward, she needed to take a breath.

She got out of the car, tasting the crisp city air as she did so. She stretched out, trying to ease the tightness in her lower back, linking her fingers together and then pressing her hands up toward the sky…

As she did so, something caught in Maya's mind. Not a full-fledged thought, just a feeling that wouldn't go away. Something about stretching…

She remembered the photograph she'd seen on Amber's social media feed. She remembered the belly button ring. It might be nothing, but her instincts were telling her then that she needed to look deeper, needed to check.

She got back in the car.

"That was quick," Marco said. "I thought for a moment that you were going to do the full Rocky thing and run up the steps."

Maya knew he was trying to lighten the mood, but she had more serious things to think about in that moment. Snatching up her laptop, Maya went back to Amber's social media feed.

"What is it?" Marco asked. "What are you looking for?"

"A sapphire navel piercing," Maya said. "It was in one of Amber's pictures. I need to know if it's in others. Because it *wasn't* in the effects the coroner found on her."

She saw Marco start to look, using his phone, but Maya was already working on it, trying to find any photos she could of Amber Kaley with a bare midriff. There was one of her at the beach in a bikini. There was another of her at a party wearing a halter top and jeans. There was another of her posing after a run. There were a lot of them. Amber was obviously proud of the body she'd built with her running and seemed happy to show it off.

In all of them, the piercing shone out, bright blue. In every photograph where Amber's stomach was bared, the piercing was there.

Even so, Maya didn't want to rush to any conclusions. She could think of at least one way of checking her hunch before she went any further. She looked up a number for Amber's sister, Erika, and called her.

"Hello?" Erika said.

"Erika, this is Agent Gray, we spoke earlier." Just a couple of hours ago. A lot had happened since then.

"What is it?" Erika asked, sounding suddenly worried. "Did you find something?"

"I was hoping that you could help me with a piece of information about your sister," Maya said. "There's a piece of jewelry she wore: a sapphire navel piercing. Do you remember it?"

"Of course I remember it," Erika replied. "It used to be one of our grandmother's earrings, but the other one got lost after she died. Amber had the idea to wear it as a navel piercing."

"So it meant a lot to her?" Maya said.

"Absolutely. She never took it off."

That was exactly what Maya had been hoping to hear, but she wanted to be certain. She needed there to be no doubt before she went down this path. There wasn't any more time to waste on blind alleys.

"Never? You're certain? She wouldn't wear it some days and leave it off others?"

"No," Erika said. "It was important to her. She said that she could feel our grandmother with her when she wore it. She *never* took it off. Look, what's this about?"

"Did anyone from the coroner's office return the ring to your family after your sister passed?" Maya asked.

"No, no, I don't think so. My parents would have said if they had it. They would know that I'd want it. To be honest, I thought about calling the cops to make sure they hadn't lost it, but… I wasn't sure who to talk to and I didn't want to cause a fuss when they were trying to find who killed her."

Meaning the police never had a chance to realize just how important that piercing was to Amber.

"Thank you, Erika, you've been very helpful. I can't say anything now, but I'll call you if I find out more."

Maya hung up, looking over to Marco.

"She wore the same sapphire ring in her navel at all times, but there's no mention of it in the coroner's report."

"Could it have been lost in the file, or just not noted down?" Marco asked.

Maya shook her head. She could feel her excitement rising again as the prospect of a lead to follow came into view.

"No, I don't think so. It has other pieces of jewelry in it, and you've seen the rest of the work here. It was thorough. This is big-city policing, not some small town where it might be overlooked."

"But this piece of jewelry isn't there," Marco said, obviously understanding the implications of that. "Meaning that either someone at the coroner's office was very sloppy…"

Maya nodded. "Or the killer took the piercing."

CHAPTER THIRTEEN

Maya called ahead, because she didn't want to waste time trying to find Detective Tanner once she got to their destination. Maya hadn't been planning to go anywhere near Philadelphia's PD, but now she found that she needed to, if she was going to get the answers she wanted.

"Are you sure you want to bring them into this?" Marco asked as they pulled up outside the station that held Detective Tanner and his homicide department. He was obviously thinking about some of the delays that had come when they'd involved local law enforcement in the past. Even in Cleveland, where Maya had had his help, there had still been problems with his bosses not wanting the FBI in town.

"I don't think we have a choice," Maya said. "I need to check this against the local police database, not just the FBI ones."

Maya knew she needed to at least talk to Detective Tanner, because she suspected now that this case might be even bigger than it had first seemed.

She walked into a busy reception area, filled with the usual mix of uniformed officers bringing people in, angry people there to complain about crimes, and people who were obviously there to speak to one of the detectives. Most of them were crammed into uncomfortable wooden chairs, and at least half of them seemed to be shouting at one another.

It was a long way from the ordered cleanliness of the FBI headquarters, but then, they didn't have to deal with local drunks or minor pickpockets protesting their innocence.

"Agent Gray!"

A man who must have been Detective Tanner was there in the reception area, waiting for her. He was a square-jawed man in his forties in a cheap sports jacket, with a muscular frame running slightly to fat and intelligent eyes that suggested that Maya shouldn't underestimate him.

Maya went over.

"You can spot that I'm FBI just by looking at me?" Maya asked.

"I googled you," he replied. That came with a faint smile. It disappeared quickly. "I thought you weren't planning on me even seeing you while you were here in Philadelphia."

"Things have changed," Maya said. She gestured to Marco. "This is Detective Spinelli. He works with me on the taskforce I head."

It was still strange hearing herself tell someone that she was in charge of a taskforce. Maya had never sought authority in her career, never pushed for promotion, but now she had everything that came with being a leader.

"So what brings you here?" Detective Tanner asked.

"I found some evidence in the Amber Kaley case that worries me, and I need you to check it against your local databases."

"What kind of evidence?" Detective Tanner asked.

Maya looked past him. "Can we go somewhere? I don't want to do this in your reception area."

She didn't want to raise her suspicions there, in the middle of the crowded reception area. It was the kind of thing she didn't want to get into the press, and she was sure that anything she said too loud *would* make it into the press. It was the kind of thing that might cause a panic, and that kind of panic would only make it harder for her to conduct her investigation.

Worse, it might tell whoever had done this that someone had worked out what they'd done. It would give them a reason to run, rather than continuing to go about their life, thinking they'd gotten away with it.

Some of that must have come through on Maya's face, because Detective Tanner nodded and led the way upstairs, into a broad bullpen filled with detectives working through their cases. He led Maya and Marco over to a cubicle, where he sat down on an aged office chair and looked up at Maya expectantly.

"Well?"

"Something was taken from Amber Kaley's body: a blue sapphire navel piercing. Her sister has confirmed that she never took it off, but it wasn't on her when she was found dead. Someone took it."

Detective Tanner stared at her for a moment or two, then frowned.

"That's what you made me come up here to tell me? That a piercing was missing from the body?"

Maya had seen Tanner's reports; she had no reason to think that he was stupid, or a bad detective.

“Think about it, Tanner. A piercing was taken, not lost, but taken. What does that imply?”

The detective shook his head gruffly. “I’m not going to be talked through this like I’m some kind of kid. Come out and say what you want to say.”

Maya looked over at Marco. She suspected now that the detective would listen to Marco more easily than to her, cop to cop, man to man.

“Two possibilities,” Marco said, counting them off on his fingers. “Option one: the piercing was targeted to steal. That’s a possibility, because we’re talking about a valuable piece of jewelry, and it explains why nothing else was touched.”

“And option two?” Tanner said. He had to know where they were going with this, though.

“That it was taken as a trophy,” Maya said, fixing the detective with a level stare, determined to show him just how serious she was about this.

“Are you talking about a serial killer?” Detective Tanner asked. He sounded slightly offended. “It was bad enough with all the Moonlight Killer stuff, and the FBI coming down then. Do you really think that we would miss a serial killer in our city? We aren’t some small-town hicks.”

“Maybe that’s the problem,” Marco said. “How many murders do you get a year in Philly, Detective Tanner?”

“Five hundred fifty-one homicides last year,” the detective said, with a note of something close to guilt. This was obviously a man who felt that he should be able to do something to stop it all.

“In Cleveland, it was a hundred sixty-five,” Marco said.

“Are we playing ‘whose city is safer’?” Detective Tanner asked, in a not entirely friendly tone.

“No, I’m saying that big cities might have better resources and trained cops, but we also have far more deaths to deal with. Enough that a killer could get lost in the noise; that a series of murders could get chalked up as something else.”

“And that’s what you think has happened in my city?” Detective Tanner said.

“We don’t know yet.” Maya decided that was a good moment to cut in. “That’s why we need to check local case files. Either they’ll tell us that this was a one-off, in which case we suddenly know that the piercing was significant to the killer in some way, or…”

"Or I have a freaking serial killer on my hands," the detective said. Maya could hear just how worried that prospect made him. She saw him nod. "All right, I'll pull up the case files at my computer, and you can try to work your way through them. If you need anything… well, you said it yourself, Detective Spinelli: we get a lot of murders in Philadelphia, and I have my own work to get on with."

It wasn't the kind of open, helpful cooperation Maya might have dreamed of, but it also wasn't the kind of outright obstruction that she'd faced elsewhere. If it meant that Maya got to actually check the records, then Detective Tanner walking away and leaving her to it was fine.

She was sure he would come back if she found that there actually was a serial killer at work.

Was there, though? Marco had set out both possible scenarios to the detective, and right then, Maya wasn't sure which of them was correct. She didn't have enough evidence either way. That was why she needed to look at the files.

She set to work, with Marco beside her. They started to go through the files, and Maya realized in moments that there simply wasn't enough time to go through every file in detail. Even for just this year, there were hundreds, and if she went back further to try to find a killer who had been at work since before they killed Amber, it would be far, far more. That was a good way to use up all of their remaining time, and still not find the killer.

Instead, she tried to narrow it down using a search for any cases that involved jewelry. There was a danger in that, of course: Amber's case proved that missing jewelry wasn't always spotted by the investigators, simply because they didn't know it was supposed to be there.

Still, the search started to turn up possible results. Too *many* possible results. There was no way they could all be related to one murderer. Maya needed to find a way to narrow them down. She started by eliminating the ones where there had been a conviction, mostly robberies that had gotten out of control, or people who had killed family members or friends over some expensive piece of jewelry that they thought should have been theirs.

Momentarily, Maya found herself thinking of Erika. Was it plausible to suggest that Amber's sister might have thought the former earring should have come to her? Maybe, but if so, why hadn't she brought it up with the police at the time? The easy way to get it wasn't to take it from her sister's corpse, meaning that she could never wear it, but to simply wait for Amber's property to be returned to her family.

In any case, Maya had seen how much Erika wanted her to find the truth in this. She didn't think it was the sister.

Who, then? Maya tried to narrow it down more, looking at the unsolved cases and discounting those where other things had been taken alongside jewelry. That still left several cases, all involving high-value jewelry, prominently displayed. There didn't seem to be any pattern to the killings, though. They were in different locations around the city, at different times, without an obviously repeating time period between them. Was it really possible that one killer was responsible for all of them? If so, they'd been killing for years, and no one had noticed. There had to be some other way to narrow things down further.

Even while Maya was thinking about it, a young female detective walked up to the desk Maya and Marco were working at. She was black, shorter than Maya, maybe five-six, solidly built, with short spiked hair and a silver stud in her left ear. She had a no-nonsense look to her, as if she'd put up with a lot of nonsense trying to make detective, and wasn't going to take any more now.

"You Agent Gray?" she asked.

Maya nodded and stuck out a hand, trying to be professional. "And you are?"

The other woman shook it. She had a strong grip, and she looked Maya dead in the eyes while she did it. The kind of determined handshake Maya knew well, because she'd had to develop one herself to deal with men who insisted on showing how strong they were when they first shook hands.

"Detective Angela Dunlop. I just saw Tanner down by the coffee machine."

"And Detective Tanner sent you my way?"

Detective Dunlop shrugged. "Kind of. He told me you're looking into cases where jewelry has been taken from murder scenes, but nothing else was taken."

"That's right."

"Well, I think I have something for you then. A murder just yesterday: Clarissa Peavey. Killed by a single stab wound to the chest. Her blue diamond engagement ring was taken from her, but nothing else."

Maya looked over at Marco. That sounded too much like Amber's death for it to be a coincidence.

"Tell me about the case," she said to Detective Dunlop.

"I'll do one better than that," the detective said. "I'm going to talk to the victim's fiancé, Hank Neushauer, right now. You can tag along if you want."

Maya didn't hesitate. "Lead the way."

CHAPTER FOURTEEN

Maya had to admit that Hank Neushauer's home was impressive. A mansion set in its own grounds within the Chestnut Hill area of the city, built of gray stone with white marble pillars out front, it was the kind of place that suggested wealth on a scale that Maya generally didn't run into.

It also meant that she was going to have to be polite about this. As the head of her own unit, she didn't have Harris to deflect any trouble from her now, and there wasn't enough time for Maya to waste in dealing with complaints from someone important. She would have to tread carefully.

She and Marco pulled up in front of the house, next to Detective Dunlop's car. Maya let the detective lead the way up to the house, and she wasn't entirely surprised to find a uniformed butler opening the door to them, showing them into an entrance hall that was significantly larger than Maya's apartment back in DC.

"Detective Dunlop, Mr. Neushauer has been expecting you. Your companions are…"

Maya answered for herself. "Maya Gray, FBI. This is Detective Spinelli."

"FBI? If you would care to wait here, I shall inform Mr. Neushauer at once."

The butler hurried back into the house, leaving them there for a minute or so, presumably while he conferred with his boss. Maya wasn't used to being left waiting like that, but she used the time to look around at the mansion that surrounded her.

There were paintings on the walls, mostly landscapes, but also a few portraits of people who might have been Mr. Neushauer's ancestors. Most of the interior was painted white, so bright that it almost seemed to glow, and the chandelier overhead dripped with crystals that caught the light.

"Mr. Neushauer will see you all in the library," the butler said, as he returned. "If you will follow me?"

He led the way through to the kind of library that a small college might have been proud of, set over both a ground floor and a mezzanine, with shelves reaching from floor to ceiling. There were plinths set among it all with artworks on top of them, while comfortable chairs were placed between them. A man who must have been Mr. Neushauer sat in one of those chairs, with a trio of others put in place in front of him, obviously ready to receive Maya and the others.

Hank Neushauer was in his early thirties, sharply dressed in a navy pinstripe suit and open-necked shirt, with quarterback good looks, blond hair, and pale blue eyes. Maya could see the signs of grief weighing heavily on him, from the effort it obviously took to wave the three of them forward to the button of his shirt that wasn't fastened correctly, as if he hadn't been able to focus long enough to do it right.

"Please, sit down," he said, gesturing to the chairs. He looked over at Maya. "Hall says that you're with the FBI? Why is the FBI involved in this? Is that because of who I am?"

Perhaps he thought that whatever importance and money he had meant that additional resources had been brought to bear. Maya wanted to think that the murder of the most unnoticed homeless person would get the same attention, but she wasn't naïve enough to believe that cases involving the wealthy didn't get additional resources thrown at them. These were the people who could throw funds at someone's campaign for DA, or who might already have contributed a lot to the local police department.

"No, Mr. Neushauer," Maya said. "I'm here because of a possible link to another case."

"For the moment, why don't we focus on the basics?" Detective Dunlop said. "Did your fiancée have any enemies, Mr. Neushauer?"

"What? No, of course not. Certainly no one disliked her enough to do something like *this*."

"Even so, it would be good to have a list of the people she knew, so that we can eliminate them from our inquiries."

Maya knew it was the stuff the detective was supposed to do, but she found herself feeling certain that it wasn't where they were going to find answers in this case. She asked the questions she actually wanted answers to, instead.

"Tell me about the engagement ring you gave her," Maya said.

Hank Neushauer looked at her as if he didn't quite know what to say. "Why do you want to know about it?"

"The ring was taken from the crime scene," Marco put in. "If we know more about it, it might help us."

"Do you think that's the reason my Clarissa was killed? Was this some kind of robbery? I wanted to give her the best. She deserved the best. But if it's the whole reason she was killed, then…"

Maya could hear the guilt there. She guessed that Hank Neushauer was currently blaming himself for making his fiancée a target, for putting her in harm's way. Maya could understand that feeling, because it was exactly what she felt when it came to her sister, Megan. Without Maya, Megan wouldn't currently be in the hands of a serial killer.

"I know what it's like, blaming yourself," Maya said. "But this *isn't* your fault, Mr. Neushauer, and the best thing you can do now is to help us to find whoever did this."

"I'll do whatever I can, obviously."

Maya asked the question that she'd wanted to ask since she walked in the door.

"Did Clarissa ever mention a woman by the name of Amber Kaley?" she asked.

"Who is that?" Hank Neushauer replied.

"Someone else who was killed," Maya explained. "Do you know if Clarissa knew her? She was a nurse at the university hospital here."

She saw Hank Neushauer thinking for a moment or two, and Maya appreciated that. She wanted him to be sure.

"No, I don't think she ever mentioned anyone by that name. I didn't really know all of her friends, but I don't think she knew anyone from the hospital. Clarissa worked in marketing."

So there was no reason why they might have met. Maya sat back, letting Detective Dunlop continue with her questions.

"Why was she at the bar in Center City?" the detective asked. "Bar 7?"

"Oh, she was out with a few of her friends, celebrating our engagement."

"And was this celebration planned?"

That was a good question.

"I think so, yes. In any case, it's a bar Clarissa goes to… *went* to, pretty regularly."

Meaning that it didn't have to be a crime of opportunity. Someone could have seen her there, seen the ring, and decided what they were going to do ahead of time.

Maya waited while the detective finished her questions, and then stood, shaking Mr. Neushauer's hand.

"Thank you for your time."

She and Marco followed Detective Dunlop out of the house.

"I need to get back to the station to write this up," Detective Dunlop said. "What do you plan to do now, Agent Gray?"

The answer to that was simple.

"I want to take a look at Bar 7."

*

Maya and Marco drove back into town, parking as close as they could get to the bar. She couldn't see any signs of a crime scene there, suggesting that a CSI unit had already been over it thoroughly, picking it clean of any evidence.

It was only midafternoon, but the place was lit up. A bouncer stepped in the way as Maya and Marco approached. He was a large, shaven-headed man in slacks and a sweatshirt, with silver chains around his neck. He held up a hand.

"Sorry, folks, we're not open this afternoon. We'll be open again later tonight."

Maya held up her ID. "FBI. What's your name?"

"Tommy." He didn't offer up a last name.

"Were you working the door last night?"

The big man looked her up and down, then nodded. "You're here to ask questions about what happened?"

"We are," Marco said. "Did you see Clarissa Peavey last night?"

"The woman who was killed? Kind of hard to miss her, you know? Her and her three friends don't exactly hold back when they're here."

"Did they come in here a lot?" Maya asked. That was potentially important. If someone had seen Clarissa there several times, maybe that would be enough for them to start planning how to kill her.

"Sure. Every few nights."

"And Clarissa was showing off her engagement ring last night?"

"Of course she was," Tommy said, as if it were obvious that she would be. "A woman like that wasn't going to hold back on being the center of attention."

Maya looked around, spotting the camera above the door. "This place has security footage?"

Tommy nodded. "The cops have been through it, though. They didn't see anything."

"I still want to take a look, if that's OK?"

Tommy shrugged. "You'll have to ask management."

He stepped back to let Maya and Marco inside, going in with them. The interior of the club was bright and colorful, with plenty of lighting set around the place and huge speakers at the front. Most of it was either dance floor or bar, but there were booths set around the edges of the floor.

An overweight man in his fifties sat in one of those booths, drinking and looking worried.

"Hey," he said. "You can't be in here. We're—"

"FBI," Maya said, showing her ID once more. "Are you the manager here?"

"Steve O'Neil," he replied. "I run the place. Although I don't know how much longer that will continue after someone was murdered outside."

"Do you have security footage of that night?" Maya asked.

He nodded. "Sure. Tommy, show it to them."

Maya looked over to Marco. "You go through it. Look for anyone following Clarissa out of the bar, or showing more interest than they should in her engagement ring. I want to ask Mr. O'Neil a couple of questions."

Marco nodded. "If there's anything, I'll find it."

Maya knew he would. He headed off with the bouncer, into a back room behind the bar.

"Drink?" the bar manager asked Maya.

She shook her head. "Not while I'm working."

"Well, I'm going to, even if you don't." He took another swig of his drink. "What questions do you want to ask me?"

"Were you out on the floor the night of the murder?" Maya asked.

"Some of the time, sure. I had to do a few things in back as well."

"But you saw Clarissa Peavey?"

He nodded. "Sure."

"Did you see anyone looking at her, anyone giving her more attention than they should have?" Maya asked.

"I mean *everyone* was paying attention to her. No one stood out more than anyone else, though."

Maya wondered how much she should take the bar manager's word for it. Probably, he had plenty of experience seeing when there was going to be trouble in his bar.

"Can you show me the rest of the bar?" Maya asked.

The bar manager shrugged. "Whatever."

He stood, leading her around.

"This is the booth where they were." It was off to one side, but there would have been a pretty good view of it from the rest of the bar. Someone could have picked her out as a potential target from almost anywhere in the room.

The bar manager led the way over to the bar.

"I don't think I saw her up here all evening," he said. "Her friends were buying the drinks. Well, them and the guys hoping to catch their attention."

"Did anyone stand out?" Maya asked. "Did any of them talk to Clarissa?"

The bar manager shook his head. "She didn't seem to be paying any of them any attention. With that big engagement ring on her finger, I guess she was making it clear that she was off the menu, you know?"

Marco came back out into the main bar area.

"There's no sign of anyone following Clarissa when she left the bar. There's a camera on the exit, and it would have caught them."

Which suggested that whoever killed her had been waiting outside the bar, rather than targeting her within it. Unless…

"Are there any other exits to this place?" Maya asked the bar manager.

"There's one at the back, but that's employees only."

"And does *that* have a camera on it?"

The bar manager shrugged. "Never saw the point. I told you, it's employees only."

Which would be fine as an answer if Clarissa was killed by one of the customers in the bar, but what about if she'd been targeted by one of the employees? Was it possible that someone who worked here was the one killing people and taking their jewelry?

CHAPTER FIFTEEN

The first thing Maya wanted to do was to establish if the bar had any link to Amber. They were potentially looking for someone who had killed multiple people, after all, and that only made sense if she had been there.

She pulled up a photograph of Amber on her phone, holding it out to the bar manager.

"Have you ever seen this woman before?"

"What?" he said. "What is this woman, a suspect?"

"A murder victim, from about a year ago. Her name was Amber. Do you remember her ever coming to your bar?"

"I don't have the best memory for faces," the bar manager said, which didn't answer Maya's question one way or the other. She needed something far more definitive from him.

"Tommy!" Marco called out.

Maya frowned. "Why are you shouting for the bouncer?"

"Door security remember faces. They have to, if they're going to remember who's trouble and who isn't, who gets too drunk, who got barred last time around."

That was the difference between live and cold cases. Marco probably spent far more time talking to that kind of security staff than Maya did.

The bouncer came to join them and the bar manager, looking as if he was worried that he was about to be accused of something.

"What?" he asked.

"Have you ever seen this woman in the bar?" Maya asked, holding up a picture of Amber. "Probably at least a year ago. Maybe with people from the university hospital."

Tommy stared at the picture for several seconds, face screwing up in concentration as he did so.

"Yeah, I guess," the bouncer said at last. "I think she was in here with a bunch of nurses. They always used to drink pretty hard, but I guess it's a stressful job. Never caused any trouble."

So, there was a good chance that Amber had been in there. They would have to check the security footage to be certain, assuming it went back that far, or search through Amber's social media for footage of her at the bar, but for now, it was enough to move forward with.

Did it mean anything, though? A bar like this was a popular local spot. It *could* just be coincidence that both Amber and Clarissa had been here. Even so, Maya decided to at least check out the possibility that it had been more than that.

"Have you ever had any trouble with your employees?" Maya asked the bar manager.

"Are you kidding? This is a *bar*, lady."

"Agent," Marco said, from beside Maya, in a tone that made it clear he wasn't going to let the bar manager get away with any disrespect.

Maya appreciated the sentiment, but she was more focused on the case than that.

"Meaning what?"

"Meaning that we get casual staff moving through. Meaning that we don't always get the nicest people working here."

"And have any of them ever caused any *particular* trouble?" Maya asked. She wanted to narrow things down. "Have any of them ever caused trouble with women like the two victims?" She thought for a moment about the jewelry. "Have any of them ever been caught stealing from customers?"

The bar manager flinched at that, and Maya knew he must have thought of a possible name for her.

"Who?"

"There's a guy works here. Vincent. Look, I'm not saying anything ever happened for sure, but I've had a couple of complaints about things going missing from tables when he's been working. A phone, a watch, you know? I never really had enough proof to call him out on it."

"And was Vincent working two nights ago?" Marco asked.

The bar manager nodded.

Meaning that he might have seen Clarissa flashing her expensive engagement ring around. He might have decided to take it from her. He might have stabbed her for it. It was quite a leap from picking up an unattended cell phone to murder, but if only an employee would have had access to the exit without a camera on it, Maya knew she had to check it out.

"I need Vincent's full name and address, right now."

*

It turned out that Vincent Westridge's apartment was walking distance from the bar, so Maya and Marco headed over there on foot, moving as quickly as they could.

"Do you really think this is our guy?" Marco asked.

Maya shrugged. "If we assume that this was about stealing expensive items, then he's a plausible suspect. We know both victims visited the bar. We know that if someone followed Clarissa out of there, it was through an employees' only exit. A member of staff is the obvious choice here, and if we now know that there's one who is probably stealing from customers, he's our best shot."

"It might still be something else," Marco pointed out. "You said yourself that taking the jewelry might be about taking trophies, not stealing. And the killer *could* have been waiting outside the bar, the same way Amber's killer waited to ambush her on her running route."

Those were both valid points, but Maya still wanted to check out Vincent Westridge.

"Either way, this is a lead we need to at least look at," Maya said. "Maybe we look at him, and he's our killer, or maybe we manage to eliminate him as a suspect. We definitely can't just ignore this."

"I'm not suggesting that we do," Marco said. He glanced at his watch, though. The message wasn't lost on Maya. She was more aware than anyone of the way time was ticking past. How many more dead ends could they look at today, and still have enough time to catch the killer?

Vincent Westridge's building was a small redbrick apartment building, built over four floors. His name was on one of the buzzers by the door, and Maya pressed it, hoping to be let in.

"Who is it?" a man's voice answered.

"Vincent Westridge?" Maya said. "This is Agent Maya Gray, with the FBI. I'm here to talk to you about the death at the bar the other night."

She tried not to inject any note of accusation into her words. For the moment, at least, she wanted to make it sound as if she were just going around talking to witnesses.

"Vinny isn't here right now," the voice said.

Was that Vincent, pretending he wasn't home in order to avoid talking to her?

"Who is this, then?" Maya asked.

"I'm Jake, Vinny's roommate."

Maya looked over to Marco, who shrugged. It seemed that it was her decision what the two of them did next. They could go away and try to find something else to do while they waited for Vincent to come back, or…

"May we come in anyway?" Maya asked. "I'd like to talk to you about Vinny."

There was a pause on the other end of the line.

"I guess. Third floor."

The roommate buzzed them in. Maya saw that the interior was pretty dilapidated, mail piling up in some of the mailboxes near the door and plaster cracked on the ceiling. A set of stairs lay ahead, and she headed up to the third floor with Marco in her wake. One of the doors there was open, with a young man in his early twenties standing next to it.

He was skinny and bearded, with shoulder-length dark hair. He was wearing jeans and a T-shirt for a band Maya hadn't heard of, not that that necessarily meant anything. There were plenty of bands she didn't know anything about. Judging by the spiky lettering and skull motif on the shirt, Maya guessed that it was some kind of hard rock or metal thing.

"You must be Jake," she said. She gestured to Marco. "This is Detective Spinelli. May we come inside to talk to you?"

He stepped back out of the way, letting them into an apartment that was quite clearly home to two single guys. The mess was one clue, with old pizza boxes pushed into neat piles by the main room's couch, as if that counted as tidying up. An electric guitar sat propped against the couch, while the TV in front of it had a games console hooked up, paused partway through a game.

"Where is Vincent?" Maya asked, trying to determine if he would be back soon.

"He's at work," Jake said. "He works at a department store during the day, then in the bar at night."

So he was working two jobs to try to make ends meet. Did that mean that he was short of money? Did that fit with the idea of someone who killed to take expensive jewelry, or did it just mean that he was desperate enough to do so? Maya still wasn't sure.

"Have you ever seen him acting suspiciously?" Maya asked.

She saw Jake shrug. "I don't know. I mean, what's suspicious? He's a cool enough roommate. Lets me get on with my music. Doesn't wake me up when I'm trying to sleep."

"Has he ever left at odd hours?" Marco tried.

"I mean, he works two jobs."

Maya tried a different tack. "Has he ever mentioned the names Amber Kaley or Clarissa Peavey?"

That just got a shrug from the young man. "Why would he?"

Maya realized then that she wasn't going to get much out of a roommate who obviously didn't spend that much time around Vincent. Certainly, Vincent wasn't about to confess anything he'd done to his friend.

Maya needed to do things a different way. She leaned in close to Marco.

"Distract him."

Marco frowned at her, obviously guessing what she was planning next.

"Is this a good idea?" he asked.

"I need to look around. Distract him."

Marco looked as though he might argue more, but then nodded. "So, Jake. I need you to tell me everything you can about Vincent. Start with when you first met him…"

He put an arm around the younger man's shoulders, starting to lead him away. Maya took advantage of the distraction to move deeper into the apartment, hunting for Vinny's room, moving as quickly and as quietly as she could.

"I just need to use your bathroom," she called out, to cover herself.

It was fairly easy to tell which room was Vinny's, and which room was Jake's. Jake's was the one with the band posters and the faint smell of weed hanging in the air. Vinny's was the neater of the two, although it still looked as if he came and went from it in a hurry every day.

Maya did her best to search it quickly, looking for any sign of anything connected with the case. She opened drawers and looked through them, shutting them behind her. She looked into a wardrobe, quickly checking the pockets of a couple of jackets there.

She glanced under the bed, and that was when she saw the cigar box sitting there. Maya didn't know Vinny, maybe he did smoke cigars, but if so, why hide the box under his bed like that? Just its presence there struck her as instantly suspicious.

Taking it out, Maya opened it, trying to touch it as little as possible.

Maya found her excitement rising as a small treasure trove of objects greeted her. There was a phone that was obviously the one that had been taken from the bar. There was a watch, too, expensive looking and Swiss made. There were a few items of jewelry.

Maya couldn't see either the piercing or the ring, but maybe that just meant that Vincent had been able to get rid of them already. With no time to search further, she put the box back carefully and then hurried back out to where Marco was still talking to Jake.

"...and which department store did you say that Vinny works at?"

"Johnson's, just a couple of blocks over."

"Thank you, Jake, you've been very helpful," Maya said, as she came back up to the two of them.

"Is that it?" Jake asked. "You don't want to know anything else?"

"We might want to talk to you again," Maya said. "For now, though, I think Detective Spinelli and I need to pay Vincent a visit at work."

CHAPTER SIXTEEN

Frank was waiting to make a phone call. He'd always had a number of ways of communicating with the outside world. When it came to dear Maya, he kept it strictly to his postcards, both because they seemed to be the mode of communication that would have the greatest effect on her and because the sheer simplicity of it avoided the FBI's resources in a way that phone calls or electronic communications wouldn't.

Even with most of the people he had do things for him, he normally kept to the postcards, delivered by people who did not dare to cross him, or who did not know what they were handing over. In a lot of cases, they were sufficient. A threat, a demand, and people did what he required.

But they were not good when it came to more… nuanced communication. They didn't provide good routes for a contact to relay information back to him. Nor did they allow him to provide complex instructions in real time.

For this, there was a very simple problem: he needed to be able to talk to his contact in the lead up to his acquisition of Claire Rainford. That mean telephone communication, rather than anything written. If his contact were a more tech-savvy man, that might represent a risk, but as it was, Frank was confident that he could remain safe throughout this.

That was why he was currently sitting in the command room of his bunker, a burner cell set up next to a voice scrambler. His contact would be waiting, had been *told* to wait, on the postcard that had accompanied the phone he'd sent.

Frank called that phone now. It rang three times before his contact picked up.

"Hello, Lee," Frank said. The voice scrambler took the words and turned them into something that could never be recognized as his without sophisticated audio decryption equipment.

"Who is this?" a man's voice on the other end of the line demanded.

"There's no point in trying to sound tough, Lee," Frank said. "It won't work on me, and it might land you in trouble. I take it you saw the pictures loaded on the phone? I can send you fresh copies if needed."

The pictures in question showed Lee Gibbons in the middle of robbing a home while the owners were out. Frank had taken them himself, while he'd been out stalking a different victim. He'd thought that they might come in useful one day.

Frank was good at collecting useful things. Just look at his bunnies. He thought ahead. He *planned* ahead. It was far better, and far safer, than trying to react in the moment.

"You bastard, I'll—"

"You won't do anything except what I say, Lee. Because if you *do* decide to do something other than what I say, then the pictures are going straight to the police, along with a neat description of what you were up to that night. You'll go back inside, and this time, it will be for good, won't it?"

There was no answer from the other end of the line. Frank smiled faintly to himself.

"If you do what I want, though, there will be payment. Generous payment."

It was important to have a carrot as well as a stick in these situations. A man like Lee might do something stupid if there were only threats to keep him in line. His greed, though… his greed could be *relied* upon. The only reason Frank hadn't just offered him money was the fact that so many ordinary people seemed to balk at the things he asked them to do.

With this, he needed to be sure.

"What do you want me to do?" Lee asked.

There wasn't enthusiasm there, exactly, but at least there was a feeling that he would do what Frank wanted. That was all Frank required. All he *ever* required. People didn't have to like their part in his plan, just as long as they did what was needed.

"What I require is simple. There is a woman in your city named Claire Rainford. Her address is on the postcard I sent you. You will follow her. You will watch her. You will assess the security around her, and find times when she is alone. You will not approach her. You will not act. You will simply watch and report."

"What do you want with her?" Lee asked.

Was he going to pretend to have a conscience given what he did for a living? Frank would have found that almost amusing, if he weren't engaged in such a serious business.

"Consider carefully whether you want an answer to that question," Frank said. "What *you* want is to be paid, and to stay out of jail."

"Yeah, I guess," Lee replied.

"No," Frank snapped, firm with his new helper now. The voice scrambler took away some of the coldness of his tone, but most of it still came through. "There is no guessing. You will do this. You will not mess up. You will not go to the police. You will not talk about this with anyone. I found you in the middle of one of your little thefts, Lee. Do you think that there is *anywhere* I cannot get to you if you mess this up?"

"How… how do I tell you what I find?" Lee asked. "Do I call you?"

"You do not. From now until I contact you again, you will spend your time watching Claire Rainford. I will know if you skip even a minute. When the time is right to act, *I* will call *you*. Keep this phone by you at all times."

Frank ended the call, setting down the phone. Carefully, he removed the SIM card and snapped it, ready to be disposed of.

He sat back in his chair, watching his screens, the sight of his bunnies moving around the bunker soothing, at least. He disliked having to delegate something like this to someone so… small, but it was necessary if he was going to keep an adequate watch on his charges. A man like Lee Gibbons was as far beneath Frank as an ant was, but he still had his uses.

At least dear Maya seemed to be making progress with her own efforts. Two days was a deliberate challenge, but it was one that she seemed to be rising to. Frank didn't have a full identity for this killer, just a general idea. Maybe she would be able to fill in the blanks for him.

And, by the time she had it all worked out, Frank hoped to have a replacement bunny in hand, ready to release to her.

CHAPTER SEVENTEEN

Johnson's was about as large and old a department store as Maya had seen, occupying most of a large building in the center of town. It was the kind of place that was just worn enough to suggest history rather than dilapidation, and that in turn suggested something more upmarket than the average chain department store.

This was the kind of place that Philadelphia's wealthier residents might go to buy everything they needed, at least when they weren't having it delivered by a personal shopper.

Maya stared at the window displays, with their elegantly expensive dresses and their glittering jewelry.

"Do you think that working somewhere like this might have been a part of it?" she asked Marco.

"What do you mean?"

"Working here, seeing all these fancy things? We've seen how Vincent Westridge lives. Maybe some part of him couldn't stand seeing people who had more money than him showing it off while he was working two jobs to live *there*."

She saw Marco shrug. She guessed that Vincent's motives were less important to him right then than just the question of whether he was the killer they were looking for.

"It doesn't excuse anything. I'm not even sure it really explains anything," Marco said.

"You're not interested in the reasons people commit the crimes they do?" Maya was a little surprised by that. She knew Marco was a good detective, and she'd assumed that a part of that was some capacity to go deep into cases and understand the people involved.

"I'm interested if it lets us catch them," Marco explained. "Beyond that? There are plenty of people in the same situation as this guy. Not all of them kill people."

"No, but understanding this killer's motives might help us catch him quicker," Maya said.

Marco gestured to the front door, staffed by a liveried greeter. "If you're right about Vincent Westridge, then we're just about to do that regardless of his motives."

If it was him. Maya was pretty confident at this point, having seen the trinkets that he'd collected from people, but she knew they needed more evidence than that. They would need to question him, and try to get something from him that could tie him definitively to one of the murder scenes. That would be hard, if he was determined not to talk and they only had a little time to do it.

How far would Maya go to get answers? It was a question that she'd asked herself a lot, recently, because it seemed that, with her sister's life on the line, she would do almost anything she had to. It was as if some fragment of her old military training had kicked in, where the goal was to complete the mission, almost regardless of what it took to do it. It was an instinct that had helped to keep her alive in her time in the Middle East, but as an investigator, it was a long way from the meticulous care and attention to the rules that she'd developed while working cold cases.

For now, though, they still had to find Vincent. Maya and Marco headed inside, with the greeter at the door holding it open for them both to enter.

"Good afternoon. Welcome to Johnson's. What are you both shopping for today?" the greeter asked.

Maya showed her ID. "We're looking for Vincent Westridge."

The greeter took a step back, looking slightly disappointed, as anything that didn't involve a sale wasn't worth his time. "One of the managers will be able to help you. They should be able to page him."

"Thank you," Maya said, and stepped into the place.

It was vastly more impressive inside than outside. The whole place was deliberately upmarket, everything precisely arranged, with no sense that everything was piled as high as possible to get the maximum amount of stock in at once. On the ground floor, Maya could see a large food court that she suspected wouldn't have anything that wasn't artisan, handmade or organic, a cosmetics section on a scale that could have handled the makeup for a feature film, and a tailor's with racks of suits arranged according to subtle gradations of color and style. Escalators and glass-fronted elevators provided routes up to the floor above, and down to a basement level whose sign promised luggage and travel accessories. The sales staff all wore suits or dark dresses, looking more like they were there for some kind of formal dinner than to sell things to the public.

Maya led the way over to one of the makeup counters, because it seemed to be the closest spot with staff. She picked out the manager there in a couple of seconds: a dark-haired woman in her forties elegantly made up and looking over the top of delicate lilac glasses at Maya.

"Can I help you, ma'am?" she asked as Maya approached. "Oh, yes, I see that I can. Come take a seat, and I'll have one of our salespeople show you what might be possible with just a *few* of our products!"

Somehow, the woman achieved the trick of being bright and friendly while also telling Maya that her own lack of makeup was somehow an utter embarrassment to be corrected at once. Maya had known plenty of women like her, who took things like Maya's casual dressing, or her choice of job, almost as a personal affront.

Marco seemed pretty amused by it, at least until the woman spoke again.

"And I'm sure your boyfriend would just *love* to take a whirl around our tailoring department." That came with a pointed glance at Marco's well-worn jacket.

"He isn't my boyfriend," Maya said quickly, and then, before it could get into a whole complicated conversation about what exactly Marco was to her, she held out her ID to simplify things. "Agent Maya Gray, FBI. This is Detective Spinelli."

"Just because you're in law enforcement, does that mean you can't look good while doing it?" the manager asked.

Maya pointedly ignored the question, and the implications that went with it.

"I'm looking for an employee of this department store: Vincent Westridge."

"Oooh, what did he do?" She made it sound as if she were just getting the gossip from a client. Maya, though, wasn't about to just hand over that kind of information. For one thing, she didn't want to actually accuse Vincent of anything until she'd had a chance to talk to him.

"Could you just tell me where he is, please?" she said.

The manager shrugged. "He doesn't work in my section, dear. Although I suppose I *could* call him down here.

“Could you do that, please?” Maya asked. She didn’t have any more time to waste waiting for the manager to be helpful.

“Of course.” She made it sound like a favor bestowed by a queen as she went over to a phone set on one of the counters. Her voice echoed through the department store. “Vincent Westridge to the cosmetics department. Vincent Westridge to the cosmetics department, please.”

It was direct, but Maya guessed that there was no reason why he wouldn’t do as he’d been asked. She found herself looking around the ground floor for any sign of someone coming their way.

Instead, she saw a young man descending on one of the escalators. He was middling height and average build, with a thin face and a dark goatee. His hair was cropped short. He stood uncomfortably, as if he couldn’t quite feel at home in the suit he wore for work.

Maya and Marco moved out onto the main floor to meet him, heading for the foot of the escalator. She stood there waiting, and it was only as the man who had to be Vincent stared at her that Maya realized that a guy like him who had worked in bars and who was an obvious thief would probably have the knack of spotting law enforcement. Certainly, he would be able to smell trouble when it came his way.

“FBI, Vincent,” Maya called out. “We want to talk.”

He didn’t stop to talk, but instead turned and started to run up the down escalator, moving quickly enough that he started to make ground toward the top. Maya swore to herself, looked around for the up escalator, and set off in pursuit.

She ran up onto the second floor of the store, which seemed to be dominated by kitchenware and household goods. It took her a moment to spot Vincent again, running through a display of cast iron pans, but once she did, Maya sprinted after him, dodging past the people who were just there to shop.

Maya was closing the distance, but Vincent was in among the displays now, using them for cover, keeping his head down as if he might lose her in them. Maya hung back slightly, not wanting to commit to one direction or another until she was certain which way he was going.

She saw a flash of movement going toward a spot where one of the staff was putting on a display of culinary skills to a couple of shoppers, and Maya didn’t hesitate. She ran for the display, and saw Marco closing in from the other side. Vincent was there, apparently grabbing for the first objects he could find, snatching up pots, pans, and kitchen utensils. He threw them at Maya as he backed away, forcing her to dodge as she tried to close the distance.

It slowed her advance, but it meant that Vincent didn't even see Marco coming. The detective tackled him low, his larger frame slamming into the smaller store employee and bearing him to the ground. Maya was there a second later, grabbing hold of Vincent's arm as he struggled to get free of Marco. She hauled him to his feet, holding tight as he tried to wrench clear. Marco stood too, taking his other arm, and Maya looked over to the store employee who had been giving the demonstration.

"Does this place have a back room or an office?"

The man nodded and pointed to a door off to one side, behind some of the displays. Between them, Maya and Marco pulled Vincent in the direction of that door.

"What are you doing with me?" Vincent said.

"Like I said," Maya replied, "we want to talk to you."

They headed through the door, into an employee break area that wasn't anywhere near as fancy as the rest of the building. It had a cheap table, a few plastic chairs, a kettle, and a microwave. Maya set Vincent down in one of the plastic chairs and then stood in front of him.

"I didn't do anything!" Vincent tried.

"It's a little late for that," Maya shot back. "We know about the things you took, Vincent. And you *know* we know, or you wouldn't have run."

"I don't know what you're talking about!"

An older man in the formal uniform of the staff their stepped into the room, looking flushed with anger. "Just what is going on here? A chase through the store? Manhandling one of the employees? I demand an explanation!"

Maya held out her ID.

"Who are you, please?" she asked him.

"I am James Teale, general floor manager here. FBI or not, you have no business simply grabbing one of my employees and—"

"Vincent here is a suspect in a murder investigation," Maya said. "And he ran the moment he saw us."

"Why'd you do that, Vincent?" Marco asked, from the young man's other side. "Why did you run?"

"I..." Vincent looked pale now. "Murder? I've never killed anyone!"

Maya wasn't just going to take his word for it, though. She got out her phone, pulling up pictures of Clarissa Peavey and Amber Kaley.

"You were working at the bar the other night when this woman was killed. Did you see her there, flashing her engagement ring? Did you have to have it? Did you kill her for it?"

"No, I… I didn't."

"We know about all the other things you stole," Marco pointed out. "You're the obvious suspect here, Vincent."

He looked around pleadingly. "I've never hurt anyone. OK, so I took some stuff at the bar, but… I never hurt anyone, I swear."

Maya was going to need more than his word, though. "Where were you on twenty-third of August last year, around six p.m.?"

"What?" Vincent said. "How am I supposed to remember that? Working at the bar, maybe? Or here? I don't know."

Maya looked over to the general manager. "Is there any way to check if Vincent would have been here on that date at that time?"

Mr. Teale was still looking far too angry. "A thief? I have a thief working for me?"

Maya didn't have enough time to waste any on the anger of a man who wasn't connected to her case.

"Mr. Teale," she asked again, "is there *any* way to verify if Vincent was here on the twenty-third of August last year at around six p.m.?"

"Well, we do have an automated clock in and clock out system, of course," Mr. Teale said. "Give me a moment. I'll need to check the records."

He got out an iPad and tapped at it for several seconds.

"Yes, I have records showing Vincent coming in for a later shift at two p.m. and not leaving until eight that day."

Meaning that, unless he'd found a way to slip out, he couldn't have been in the park to kill Amber.

"Is there any way he could have gotten out of here for an hour?" Marco asked.

"His absence would have been noticed," Mr. Teale said. "And a warning put on his file."

So it wasn't likely that he'd done that. Especially when Maya suspected that his boss would have been watching him carefully the whole time.

Worse, Vincent's stash didn't actually have the ring or the piercing, and that didn't fit when the killer had so obviously taken both. Taken together, both facts pointed to one conclusion: they'd caught a thief, not a killer.

They were looking in the wrong place, and now Maya had even less time to try to find a better place to look next.

CHAPTER EIGHTEEN

They returned to the police station, taking Vincent with them so that the local police could deal with his small crime spree. Maya left him as soon as they reached the front desk. She couldn't spend the next day dealing with the paperwork and the interviews for a few petty thefts when there were lives on the line.

Dunlop was waiting for them when they got there. She didn't look happy.

"Were you out following a lead on my case?"

"*Our* case," Maya corrected her. "This is linked to an active FBI investigation. Besides, the lead didn't pan out."

"You still should have let me in on what you were doing. Should have kept me informed, at least."

Was Maya going to have to report in every move she made to the detective? No, that wouldn't work. It would take too much time, slow her down too much. She didn't want to bring Dunlop along, either. Maybe she was an effective cop, but she probably wouldn't approve of some of the things Maya had been doing to try to get closer to the truth. She might even try to stop her, where Marco wasn't. *He* understood the stakes.

"I'm sorry," she said for now. "Look, there's a possible connection to your case, but we need to keep digging."

"And by that, you mean…"

"I need to go through the files on similar cases again, see if I can spot a pattern."

"*We* need to go through the files," Dunlop said, looking determined. "You're talking about this like there's some kind of serial killer in Philly, and if there is, I want to be a part of taking him down."

Was that just determination to get in on a big case that could help her career, or a kind of righteous need for justice? Either way, Maya suspected she wasn't going to get access to the files again unless she went along with it.

"All right," she said, "but I'm not waiting around for you. There's a deadline on the case I'm working, and lives are at stake if we cross it."

Dunlop gave her a look as if trying to work out how serious Maya was about that.

"We're not at liberty to talk about the details, Agent Gray," Marco said. He made it sound as if he were reprimanding her, but Maya knew that he was actually giving her a way out of having to answer difficult questions about the case. This still wasn't something that the FBI wanted to be public knowledge. If the press got hold of the fact that she was running around at the whim of a kidnapper, solving cases… or worse, if they found out who that kidnapper was…

Maya realized that she was starting to think like Harris, where a media disaster felt imminent at any moment, to be avoided at almost any cost. Maya wasn't thinking quite like that—solving the case was still her first priority—but she suspected it might put the Moonlight Killer's remaining captives in more danger if information about the case became public.

Something about the seriousness of Marco's tone must have convinced Detective Dunlop, because she nodded.

"All right. I'll help you go through the files."

They went up to the bullpen again, and this time they headed over to Detective Dunlop's desk. There were pictures of a small family there, along with a tiny cactus plant in a pot. It was a lot more homey than Maya's desk at the FBI, mostly because Maya didn't normally spend enough time at her desk to worry about making the space more personal.

Detective Dunlop called up the search feature for the police files on her computer.

"What were you looking for?" she asked.

"Any murders where jewelry was taken, but it wasn't obviously just a mugging gone wrong," Maya said. It was a little frustrating, having to talk someone else through it, when they'd already found the files once.

Still, Detective Dunlop brought up the files on her screen quickly, transferring them over to Maya's laptop, and Maya found herself scanning through them, trying to pick out the ones she wanted.

"So, no closed files," Marco said. "Nothing where a perp was caught at the scene or soon after. No obvious robbery homicides where anything other than jewelry was taken."

Slowly, the number of files started to narrow down.

"How far back did you go?" Detective Dunlop asked.

"A couple of years," Maya said. "Assuming that this is all one killer, we're talking about someone who is still active, and more recent cases are likely to be easier to look at."

"Plus serial killers don't typically have a 'career' of more than two or three years," Marco added.

That was what they were looking at now: a serial killer. It might matter in terms of catching them whether they were doing this to steal the items or for some other reason, but ultimately, there would be a pattern and evidence to lead them to the killer.

At least, Maya had to hope so.

"Let's go back two," Detective Dunlop said.

Half a dozen files came up on the screen, seeming to fit the pattern. Could they all be the work of one killer?

Maya started to read through the files, because now, there were few enough that it was the details that mattered. They'd narrowed it down enough that she could start to work through the cases one by one, looking for clues that might lead her to the killer.

"We need to look for links between the cases," she said to the others. "Try to find out if there are any obvious ways the victims are connected beyond their jewelry. Are there any locations they might all have gone to where a killer might have identified them as targets? Do they have any connections between them through social media, or work?"

"I know how to investigate, Agent Gray," Detective Dunlop said, but still, she started to work. Maya saw Marco running searches on his phone, and she looked back at her laptop and started running names through the FBI's systems.

There were six victims, not counting Amber: Clarissa Peavey, Tonya Small, Pavel Gusunov, Wendy Poole, Harvey Jacques, and Indira Singh. Six victims, killed in six different locations, but all with items of jewelry missing from them after their death. All in cases where it didn't seem that robbery had been the motive, because money had been left behind. For Amber it had been her piercing. For Clarissa, her ring. Tonya was missing a brooch, Pavel a championship ring. Wendy had a necklace taken from her, Harvey had had his watch stolen, and Indira was missing a bracelet.

It was an eclectic collection.

"There doesn't seem to be any sign that the victims were connected to one another on social media," Marco said, as he kept working. "I guess if they had been, it would have raised red flags already."

The same probably went for their jobs, but Maya checked anyway. The trouble was that it was a pretty varied selection of workplaces, too. Amber had been a nurse, and Clarissa had worked in marketing. The others were a teacher, a construction worker, a homemaker, a Realtor, and an investment banker.

Maya couldn't imagine a scenario in which they had all worked in the same place, but she still tried to think of something that might put them all in the mix. Some kind of construction project backed by Indira Singh's investment fund might do it, but one look at the site for it suggested that it specialized in tech startups, not construction. Even if the business had invested in construction projects, it would have to be a strange one to bring in a nurse and a teacher.

What about their personal lives? Maya could see from the remains of their social media that they weren't all friends, but was there some context in which they might have met one another? Maya decided to start with the obvious.

"Marco, send pictures of these victims across to the bar manager at the place where Clarissa was killed. See if he or Tommy the bouncer recognize any of their faces. I don't want to go running after other options if it turns out that they all drank there."

Marco nodded. "Will do."

"Detective Dunlop, can you think of any places where all of these people might have gone together?"

"Too many places. Football or baseball games, a show, a restaurant. The same park. The same church."

"Probably not those last ones," Maya said, glancing again at the files. "They all lived in different districts."

They all lived in different places, worked in different places, but Maya still took Detective Dunlop's point: there were too many places in any city where thousands of people would gather at a time for guesswork to narrow down a context where a killer might have spotted them all.

Maya pored through the victims' social media instead, looking for any locations that they'd tagged themselves as being in that matched up with the others. Inevitably, there were a few, but what Maya was really looking for were places that they'd visited shortly before their death.

She couldn't imagine the killer spotting them and then waiting six months before he acted.

When she threw in that criterion, she didn't get any matches.

"There doesn't seem to be anywhere that they all went where a killer might have spotted them," she said.

"And the manager just replied to my message," Marco put in. "He thinks he might have seen Pavel Gusunov one time, but not any of the others."

So it wasn't the bar. They needed to find a different way to think about this case. Maya tried to go back to basics with all of this. What did all of the victims have in common?

The jewelry. She didn't need to spend her time looking for another point of connection between them when she had already found the connection that seemed to matter most to the killer. If the jewelry was what brought the killer to each victim, then maybe it could lead Maya and Marco back to the killer.

That was easy enough to think, but Maya still needed to work out how to actually do it. She found herself looking through the list of pieces. Would the killer keep them, or was he taking them because they were high-value items? If it was the latter, then presumably he would need to sell them somewhere.

Maya guessed that at this distance in time, trying to find a ring or a watch or a bracelet or a necklace would be difficult, if not impossible. She found herself focusing in on the wrestling championship ring belonging to Pavel Gusunov. That murder was only three months ago. There was a picture of the missing ring in the file, an obviously handmade piece inset with onyx and bearing the crest of his college. There would be few if any others like it out there, meaning that there would be every chance of finding it if it was anywhere on the open market.

Was it a part of the pattern? The danger, of course, was bringing in too many cases, but this did seem consistent. A quick kill, and just the ring taken rather than money. It fit, didn't it?

Maya didn't have enough time to search through every jeweler and pawn shop in the state, though. But she knew exactly the person who *might* be able to help. She made a call.

"Hi, Samit," she said, when the tech picked up. "I need you to locate something for me."

"Sure, what is it?"

“A collage championship ring, for wrestling,” Maya explained. “It belonged to a dead man named Pavel Gusunov, of Philadelphia. I’ll send you over an image.”

“OK, Agent Gray. I’ll find it.”

Maya hung up, hoping she didn’t have to wait long.

“You really think Samit will be able to find the ring?” Marco asked.

“If it’s out there in circulation, there’s a good chance that someone will have listed it for sale online,” Maya replied. “For a piece like that, they’ll have to advertise if they want to find a buyer.”

Even as she said it, her phone announced that she’d received a message. It was from Samit, with a link to what turned out to be a pawn shop’s online inventory. They had a hit.

Now, they just needed to get to the pawn shop and find out who had sold them that ring.

CHAPTER NINETEEN

"I'm going with you."

Maya winced as Detective Dunlop said the words she'd been dreading ever since the detective had demanded to be kept in the loop. She knew she couldn't actually stop the detective, but she was determined to find a way to persuade her not to come.

"We don't know if this will lead to anything," Maya said.

"Which is why we're going to go check it out."

"All three of us?" Maya shook her head. "Even if the killer is standing right there in the middle of the pawn shop, shouting about how he did it, Marco and I will be enough to take him down."

"And if he isn't," Marco put in, obviously seeing that Maya needed backup, "then we shouldn't have all three of us pursuing the same lead. We need to split our efforts."

A frown crept over Detective Dunlop's features. It was pretty obvious what she thought about that idea. "You're just trying to cut me out so you can have the arrest for yourselves."

Maya stared at her, then laughed. She couldn't help herself. "You think this is about glory? About who gets the arrest? I get it, you want to come out of this looking good. How many homicides have you worked?"

"This is my first one."

"And you want to find the killer, not make a mess of it, but the best way to do that is to stay here and work other angles so that we cover more ground."

Even saying that, Maya wasn't certain that she'd convinced the other woman. When Detective Dunlop nodded, Maya almost breathed a sigh of relief. She certainly didn't hesitate.

"Good. Marco and I will check this out. And if we do find the killer… well, I don't care who takes the credit. You can have the arrest."

The last thing Maya needed was more conflict with local law enforcement. She just wanted to do her job, find an answer, and hopefully get another victim back unharmed from the Moonlight Killer.

*

Maya spent every minute of the thirty-minute drive to the pawn shop only too aware of the passing time. It was late afternoon now, and it felt as if they hadn't accomplished enough on their first day investigating this case.

Maya felt a hint of hope, though, that maybe they might have caught a break. The pawn shop would be legally obliged to collect information on the person who had sold the ring to it, which meant that there was every chance she and Marco would be able to find out who the killer was.

The pawn shop wasn't in a good area of the city; Maya could see that as soon as she and Marco drove into the district. The houses looked as though they hadn't been repaired in years, and in a couple of spots, she saw the abandoned remains of burnt out cars. Her eyes caught on the figures in doorways or alleys, some of them homeless, some of them looking as though they were dealers waiting for their next clients to show up.

It was a long way from the world Clarissa Peavey inhabited, but Maya was convinced by now that the same killer had murdered both her and Pavel Gusunov.

The Dollar in Hand pawn shop was as run-down as the rest of the place, the large sign declaring its presence half obscured by graffiti. The windows had bars across them even in the daytime, so that it was barely possible to see the old guitars, TVs, and items of jewelry set out there in the displays.

Maya and Marco parked outside.

"Do we identify ourselves right away?" Marco asked.

Maya looked over at him, slightly surprised that he would be the one to suggest that. "What are you thinking we should do?"

"Maybe go in as potential customers and try to identify the ring?" Marco suggested. "Maybe get the owner to talk about it a little?"

Maya found that she liked that idea. In a place like this, there was every chance that the owner would clam up if things got too official too quickly. Maybe Marco was right, and it was better not to be too obvious about why they were really there at first.

"OK," she said. "It sounds like a good idea. We'll go in looking for the perfect gift for my father, if anyone asks. That should get us the chance to at least look around."

The two of them went in together, a buzzer sounding to announce their entrance into the store. It was harshly lit inside, which Maya didn't think was to the advantage of a lot of the items on display. It just seemed to show up all their faults, so that she saw the cracks in a set of glassware, the tarnished finish on an old side table.

The whole place was a tangle of seemingly random objects, without much in the way of order to it. Electronic goods and video games sat next to musical instruments and collections of antique coins. A large screen stood around a counter area, presumably to stop anyone jumping the counter and getting at anything there. On the wall behind it was a selection of weaponry people had traded in, mostly guns, but with a few knives, and even an antique cavalry saber.

The man who stood behind it was bald and overweight, with a walrus moustache that obscured most of the lower part of his face. He was probably an inch or so shorter than Maya, and wearing a grubby gray T-shirt and jeans emblazoned with the logo of the pawn shop. He watched the two of them with suspicion as Maya and Marco looked around the store, searching for the jewelry.

"You two looking for anything in particular?" he asked.

"We were thinking jewelry. Maybe a ring."

"Thinking of getting married?" the owner said with a small laugh as Maya felt a sudden flare of embarrassment at the thought.

Not that there would be anything wrong with being together with Marco. That was kind of the problem. It was hard to deny how attracted she was to him, and not just because he was tall, good-looking, and strong. He was also clever, a genuinely good guy, funny, and he was just *there* for her.

The owner's comment pushed at those feelings, and made Maya redden slightly in spite of herself.

"Nothing like that," Marco said. "We're looking for a gift."

"Well, the jewelry case is right there," the owner said, gesturing.

It was a big case, taking up most of a back wall. Apparently, their jewelry was the first thing that people brought in when they found themselves in financial trouble. Someone's jewelry, anyway. Maya had the feeling that this was the kind of pawn shop where the owner didn't ask too many questions about exactly where the items had come from.

Maya started to look over the jewelry. There was a lot of it, watches and brooches, pendants and bracelets. A part of her found herself wondering if the other items that had been taken from the victims might be there too. They'd just been looking for the ring taken from Pavel, but maybe there was a chance that Clarissa's ring, or Amber's piercing, might be in there too.

She worked systematically, looking up and down in a grid pattern, assessing each piece before she moved on. Maya hoped it wouldn't be too obvious, that it would just look like someone really searching for the perfect gift to give someone.

Marco was working from the other end, and Maya found herself grateful that he was someone she could trust to do it. With a lot of people, even those she worked with, Maya would have felt the need to check what they were doing, making sure that they hadn't missed anything. It was one of the reasons she'd worked alone for so long, yet here, with Marco, she felt sure that he would find the ring if it was there.

Maya spotted it first, sitting there in between a couple of necklaces, almost hidden by the glitter of everything around it. The onyx was inky black among the setting.

"This looks interesting," Maya said, pointing to it. "Could we take a closer look?"

"Sure, sure," the owner said, shifting his bulk from behind the counter with an effort. He came over and unlocked the case. "Which piece was it?"

"That one, the championship ring," Maya said, pointing.

"That one's a nice piece," the owner said, obviously trying to work out what he could get away with charging her for it.

"Where did you get it?" Maya asked. "A ring like that, it must be quite rare."

"Handmade, unique," the owner agreed.

"So where do you get something like that?"

"It's a pawn shop." The owner shrugged. "A guy brought it in. Needed the cash."

Maya looked over to Marco, silently asking if they were going to get any more out of the owner like this. He shrugged.

"What guy?" he asked.

"Why do you want to know?" the owner replied.

Maya sighed. Their brief piece of undercover work had let them establish that the ring was here, but it wasn't going to tell them more than that. They needed to do this the other way.

She took out her ID, holding it up in front of the store's owner.

"We want to know because that ring belonged to a man who was murdered, and the guy who sold you that ring is probably the killer."

Maya saw the shock flash across the owner's face, but it was brief, replaced by suspicion and hostility.

"Cops? You come in here, and you don't tell me that you're cops?"

"FBI," Maya said, "not Philadelphia PD. This isn't some local thing, and if you don't tell us who bought that ring, you could be protecting a killer."

The owner shrugged in response to that, like it didn't make any difference to him. "Or I could just be handing over information on one of my customers because you ask. I wouldn't get too many other customers if I started doing that."

It was as good as an admission that he knew that plenty of his customers weren't coming by the things they sold entirely legitimately. Except that it *wasn't* quite an admission. Certainly not enough to do anything further with.

"Is this ring really worth having this argument about?" Maya asked. "It's not like it's the most valuable piece in there."

That got another shrug from the owner. "Of course it's not. Semi-precious stone. Not even real gold. College rings rarely go for more than four hundred bucks."

"And you didn't pay close to that," Marco said, the disapproval obvious in his tone.

That just got another shrug.

"Who did you pay it to?" Maya asked, not giving up on that possibility.

The owner shook his head. "If you don't have a warrant, I'm telling you nothing."

Ordinarily, that wouldn't have been a problem. The only issue now was time. Could Maya really get a warrant quickly enough? Even if it took only hours, it might still be the setback that pushed her case past the deadline. If it took longer than that…

Maya had to find another way.

She forced herself not to show any of the frustration she felt. She forced her face to look as neutral as if this wasn't any kind of setback at all.

"OK, so we'll get a warrant. My guess is that it won't be too hard. Marco?"

She saw Marco look around pointedly, obviously getting what she was driving at.

"A place like this, I bet there have been plenty of warrants in the past. I bet the judges around here sign them the same way they sign into the building in the morning."

"And when we *do* get one, it won't just be this ring we look into," Maya said. "We'll pick apart your entire business. We'll find every dirty deal you've ever done."

Maya saw the owner swallow at that, his nerves obvious.

"Damn it. I *knew* this one would come back to haunt me."

There was another pause, and Maya let that pause drag out, letting the potential implications sink in. They obviously did.

"I give you the name and you go away?" the owner asked.

Maya nodded. "The name and the ring. My job isn't local crime. My job is to find a killer."

She heard the owner curse.

"All right, all right." He went back behind the counter for a few seconds. "I kept the paperwork, because I guessed this one might come back on me."

He held up a piece of paper.

"Here. Herb Severn. His address is on the ticket. I'm sure you can find him."

Maya took the paper from him, then went back and picked up the ring. She had a lead now.

She just had to find Herb Severn.

CHAPTER TWENTY

Maya was pretty sure that Herb Severn's apartment building was going to make her top ten worst places that she'd seen people living, and most of the ones that had been worse had been in war zones.

It was dull gray concrete, livened up by graffiti that seemed to include plenty of gang signs, although it would probably take local police to identify the exact gangs. She could see several broken windows, while a shopping cart full of trash had randomly been left on the sidewalk in front of it.

Maya was pretty sure that she and Marco were being watched as they got out of the car. She had the feeling of eyes on her, although there was still enough background noise of kids playing somewhere nearby that it didn't automatically trigger memories of ambushes from back in her army days.

"Do we call for backup?" Marco asked. "My guess is that Dunlop will be pretty pissed if we don't at least tell her."

"So we call it in," Maya said. "But we don't wait. The sooner we have Herb Severn in custody, the better."

This was potentially a very dangerous man indeed, one who'd killed just a couple of days before. Maya didn't want to risk leaving him free a moment longer than she had to.

Was she really about to solve the case, bring in the killer in one day, rather than two? Maybe *that* was why the Moonlight Killer had given her just two days for this investigation. Maybe he knew that it was more than enough time to find the man who had done all of this, once Maya found the other cases.

She didn't want to get too confident, though. She still had to catch this guy.

She called Dunlop, who picked up almost instantly.

"Agent Gray," she said. "Have you turned up anything at your end?"

"We found the guy who sold the ring," Maya said. "Marco and I are getting ready to move in."

"Text me the address. I'll be there in twenty with backup."

“It’s at least a half hour drive to the pawn shop, plus another ten to get here. Bring backup if you want, but we’re not waiting.”

“Agent Gray, that really isn’t—”

“No time to argue, Dunlop. I’ll text you the address.” Maya hung up and then sent over the address to the detective.

“She’s really not going to be happy,” Marco pointed out.

Maya shrugged. “Detective Dunlop’s happiness is not my main concern here. Catching a killer is. If we wait around out here, there’s no way Herb Severn doesn’t spot us, *especially* once the squad cars start showing up.”

She saw Marco look over the apartment block. “And if he runs, he’ll be impossible to find in a place like this.”

“Exactly. Come on. We’re going in.”

Maya led the way into the building, ignoring the slightly acrid stench of the place. Herb’s apartment was on the third floor, so they took the stairs. The elevator appeared to be out of use in any case. Now the building was quiet, and that shift made Maya reach automatically for her Glock. The whole place felt wrong, as if she and Marco might be running right into trouble.

They got to the third floor. The light there in the hall was flickering off and on with no obvious rhythm to it.

They made their way to Herb’s apartment door, and now the absolute silence around them gave way to the sound of a TV playing too loud. Someone was home. Maya hammered on the door.

“Herb Severn, open up! This is the FBI!”

There was no answer, and Maya was terrified in that moment that Herb might be on his feet, running for a fire escape. It had happened to her before, and Maya had no wish to start chasing someone through this neighborhood.

Maya nodded to Marco, and he stepped forward, kicking the door, hard. In a place like this, Maya had been half expecting some kind of barred security door, but instead, the lock broke open easily, the door bursting inward to reveal a dark, dingy apartment within.

It was a tiny square of a room with floral wallpaper stained from being there for years and a small kitchen space in the corner. There was a large TV on one wall, and a man who must have been Herb Severn sat in front of it in a ratty recliner. He was a tall, skinny guy in his thirties, with a shaved head and tattoos running up his neck onto the side of his face. He was wearing track pants and a vest, and as Maya burst in, she could see the sheer shock on his face.

"Freeze!" Maya called out, bringing up her weapon.

It didn't have any effect. If anything, the command spurred Herb into action, and he leaped out of his chair, presumably to get to some kind of weapon. For the moment, though, he was unarmed, which meant that Maya wasn't about to shoot. Yet if she waited until he *did* have a weapon, this would become life and death far too quickly.

Marco ran past her, slamming into Herb. The charge took the two of them back into the recliner, which promptly toppled under their combined weight. Maya watched the two of them wrestling with Marco trying to come out on top to hold their suspect down, and she knew she had to help. Putting her gun away, she ran forward.

She grabbed one of Herb's arms, but even then, he didn't stop thrashing and fighting. He kicked out, and Maya saw a foot catch Marco in the face, sending him back off Herb. It meant that Maya was left holding onto him alone for a second or two.

He drove up into her, his weight taking Maya over onto the ground. He loomed up over her as if he might start throwing punches. Maya managed to get her head out of the way of the first one, but a second clipped her, making pain flower at the side of her skull.

Marco was there again then, and now he was behind Herb, dragging him off Maya and pinning him to the floor. Maya didn't hesitate. She was up in an instant, moving to Herb and grabbing his left arm to wrench it behind his back. Marco got his right, and between them they managed to force his arms into a position where they could cuff him, in spite of his thrashing.

"Herb Severn," Maya said, continuing to hold him down, "you're under arrest."

*

They took Herb back to the precinct, and Dunlop was waiting for them, her expression taut with anger.

"You should have waited for backup," she said, as Maya came close.

"You're not my boss, Dunlop," Maya reminded her, "and if we'd waited, Herb here could have gotten away. Now, do you want to be a part of the interview, or are you too busy being pissed at us?"

Maya half expected Dunlop to walk away, but she seemed to get her anger under control.

"OK. Interview room three. Follow me."

She led the way to a police interview room, complete with metal table and chairs bolted to the floor, camera watching from the corner, and one-way glass on one of the walls. Maya sat Herb down on one side of the table and then took a seat on the other. There was a small recording device in the middle, so Maya set it running while Dunlop sat next to her, with Marco standing in the corner of the room.

"You're aware of your rights?" Dunlop asked him. "You have the right to have a lawyer present for this."

"You think I can afford a lawyer?" Herb snapped back. "What did all of you arrest me for? I was just defending myself. I thought it was some kind of home invasion."

Maya shook her head. "That won't work, Herb. I identified myself clearly. And claiming self-defense doesn't do *anything* about the murder charges you're looking at."

Maya saw the look of absolute terror that spread over Herb's features as she said that. Was that the fear of a man who had just realized he'd been found out, or was it something else?

"What do you mean 'murders'?" he asked.

Maya took out the ring, setting it on the table. She saw the look of recognition that flashed through Herb's eyes as he stared at it, closely followed by more of the fear that said that he knew exactly how much trouble he was in.

"I've never seen that before in my life," Herb tried.

Maya shook her head. "That doesn't work, Herb, because *this* is a pawnbroker's ticket saying that you traded it at the Dollar in Hand pawn shop. That's your name, and your address."

"Where did you get the ring, Herb?" Dunlop said.

Maya shrugged. "We already know the answer to that, don't we, Herb? You took it from the body of Pavel Gusunov after you killed him. What about the rest? What about the piercing you took from Amber Kaley, or the ring you took from Clarissa Peavey? Did you sell those to pawn shops too?"

Now Herb looked panicked. "I don't know who those people are! I only know about one body!"

"Are you confessing to the murder of Mr. Gusunov?" Marco asked from his spot in the corner of the room.

"No!" Herb insisted. "I never killed anybody."

Maya wasn't going to let it go, though. "Then why do you have the ring?"

"I… I found the body. I was out at night on my way back from a bar, and I found this guy lying in an alley. I called nine one one, but I couldn't stay. I have priors. I couldn't afford that kind of trouble."

"And yet here you are," Detective Dunlop said. "So you're saying that you stole a ring from a dead man? That's what you're saying happened?"

"It's what happened. I needed the money. I owed some people, and… it was just there, you know. I would have had his wallet, too, but I couldn't find it quick enough, and I could hear the sirens, and… that ring. I thought it was expensive, that it would solve all my problems. Turned out to be a cheap piece of trash, and all of this…"

He put his head in his hands, as if only just realizing how bad it all sounded.

"The call to the police was anonymous that night," Marco said, obviously remembering the detail from the file.

"You see!" Herb said. "That was me."

"Where were you two nights ago?" Maya asked, not wanting to let it go just yet.

"I was out of town, working," Herb replied. "I just got back. You can check with my boss."

"We will," Maya said, but her heart started to fall. "There are some other dates too. I suggest you think long and hard where you were for them."

She wrote the dates of the six murders down on a piece of paper, turning it and pushing it over to Herb.

"I'm supposed to just remember where I was?" he asked.

"If you want us to believe you, yes."

He pointed. "This one, the one in August… that one I remember. I was in Mexico for that, on vacation. Take one look at my Facebook page. The pictures are all there."

"We will," Maya said, standing.

"You know it isn't me," Herb said, looking slightly more hopeful than he had before. "Does that mean I'm free to go?"

"You stole the ring from a dead man's finger," Detective Dunlop said. "Take a wild guess."

Maya stepped outside with Marco, feeling her frustration build.

“We still haven’t checked the alibis,” Marco said, once they got out of the interview room. “They could still fall apart.”

“Maybe,” Maya replied. “But you saw the surprise on his face when I talked about more than one murder. My guess is that he had nothing to do with all this. Certainly not to do with Amber’s murder. Maybe he gets charged with something in relation to Pavel Gusunov, but all we can really prove right now is the theft. Beyond that…”

She shook her head, angry with it all.

“We don’t have anything, Marco. I thought all of this was connected, but now, now I’m starting to wonder if I have that right at all. I think we need to go back to the start. Again.”

And in the meantime, time was running out.

CHAPTER TWENTY ONE

It was dark by the time they got out of the precinct, and as much as Maya wanted to keep going with the work, she was exhausted by now. It felt as though she and Marco had chased down as many leads in one day today as they would ordinarily have gone through in three or four days.

It still hadn't gotten them their killer, though.

"We should find somewhere to stay," Marco suggested, obviously as tired as Maya was. "Maybe if we start fresh tomorrow morning, it will give us a fresh perspective on all this."

"I can keep going," Maya insisted, even though her body was telling her otherwise.

Marco shook his head. He put a hand on her arm. "Maya, even you need to rest sometimes. You have to take the time to relax. You're not going to think of anything new wound up tightly like a spring. Besides, *I'm* tired too. I don't have the stamina to keep up with you all night."

Somehow, Maya suspected that was anything but true, in any context. And just the fact that she was thinking like that made it hard to concentrate on anything other than just how close to her Marco was right then.

"We should find a motel," Marco said.

"Yes, we…" Maya managed to look away from him long enough to focus on her phone. "There's a place about ten minutes away."

They drove over. Philadelphia seemed like a very different city by night. It wasn't as easy to see any of the historic landmarks or well-kept trees in the dark, so the whole city had a more dangerous edge to it. The victims in this case had all been killed at night, and Maya found herself wondering if they'd had this sense of the danger of the city before they died, or if it had all been completely normal to them right up to the point where someone had killed them.

They reached the motel, tucked away in the middle of the city. The receptionist was a woman in her twenties, who offered them both a friendly smile as they came in.

"Hi, how can I help you? Would you like a room?"

A room. As the receptionist said that, Maya found herself thinking about all the possibilities that a single room might entail. She and Marco, sharing a room. Sharing a bed, or maybe two beds.

Except that even if the room had two beds, Maya doubted it would stay that way for long.

She looked over to Marco, and Maya could tell at a glance that he was thinking many of the same things. He'd obviously caught the reference to one room, and from the way he was looking at her, Maya knew that he was as much in two minds about it as she was.

A part of her really wanted to say yes, one room. She wanted to take this chance while it was here. She and Marco had already shown that they weren't the kind of people who went out on normal dates, so maybe it was OK that there was nothing normal about this moment either.

Maybe it was OK to just be thrown together, and then find what happiness they could. Maybe it was even better to take this chance, to see where things went, when they were far from DC, not caught up in their normal lives.

Maya could feel that part of her trying to talk her into it, and it was tempting. *Marco* was tempting. She had no doubt that if she said one room, Marco would go along with it. He'd made it clear before that he was holding back mostly because he wasn't sure that Maya was ready, that he understood that everything in this case was her priority.

The thing, though, was that the case *was* her priority. Saving her sister was the priority.

And was this really the kind of moment when Maya finally wanted things between her and Marco to go to the next level? Was this place with its kitsch décor and its perfectly repeatable franchise service really the place Maya had imagined something happening with Marco?

No, it wasn't, and the moment Maya thought that, she knew that nothing was going to happen tonight. They were both tired, both trying to focus on the case, both stressed with the limited time left to find answers. This wasn't the place for romance, in spite of the attraction that was obviously there between the two of them.

"Two rooms, please," Maya said. If there was really something there between the two of them, then there would be plenty of time to explore it when they weren't engaged in an active case, trying to find a killer.

She looked over at Marco as she said it. Did he look disappointed? Relieved? Maybe both. Certainly, he nodded along with the idea.

They paid for the rooms and headed for them. They paused at the doors, next to one another, and for a moment or two, Maya was tempted again to throw aside the idea of keeping things chaste and professional on the case. She pushed down that feeling, opening the door.

"Make sure you actually get some sleep, Maya," Marco said. "We'll start again tomorrow."

"I'll do my best," Maya promised.

*

Maya lay on the bed, unable to sleep. She stared at the ceiling in the dark, hoping that if she just lay there long enough without moving, sleep would finally claim her.

It didn't, though, because her brain wouldn't slow down enough to allow it to happen. She spent her time running through the things that had happened in this case, the ways that she hadn't been able to find answers so far.

She found herself thinking about Pavel Gusunov's death, and the ring she'd found in the pawn shop. That ring was now in the care of the Philadelphia PD as evidence, but Maya could see it perfectly in her mind's eye. She'd assumed that, as the most distinctive of the items taken from the scene of one of the murders, it would be the one that would lead them to the killer.

Except that the ring *hadn't* been taken by a killer, but by a petty thief who'd needed the money to pay off a debt. Which meant that the death couldn't be a part of the broader pattern.

Was that one of the reasons why none of this made sense? Was Maya looking for patterns in something where there was no pattern, because not all of the cases were linked?

Were *any* of them linked? Maya had come to the conclusion that a trophy implied a serial killer, but maybe it was just a one-off, and Clarissa Peavey's ring had been taken by a different killer. Maybe Maya was trying to force connections onto a situation where they didn't really exist, and only creating problems for herself in the process.

It was possible, but honestly, Maya didn't believe it. It seemed unlikely that there should be so many cases in one city where jewelry had been taken but other valuables had been left behind, where the killings had mostly been so similar in approach, with an ambush and a quick kill. Maya was sure there was a pattern there somewhere, but where?

Was it just hidden beneath the noise of cases that had nothing to do with the others? Had she confused things rather than simplifying them by introducing so many other files into the equation?

Maya didn't know, but she knew she had to find out. Getting out of bed, she flicked on the light and grabbed her laptop, dragging it back to the bed and sitting cross-legged on it while she started the computer up.

She still had the files that Dunlop had sent across to her, which meant that she could at least look at the details of the cases that she'd assumed were one group. If Maya could just eliminate some of the cases, maybe there would be a much clearer pattern that stood out to her.

Maya started by taking away Pavel Gusunov's case. As tragic as his death was, it wasn't a part of the bigger cluster. Was the other man in the group another anomaly? Maybe this was a killer who only targeted women, as so many seemed to. Maya started to read through Harvey Jacques's file, trying to find an answer, but the more she read, the more she was convinced that he *had* to be a part of the pattern. He'd been a businessman who'd been on his way to his tennis club when an unknown person had approached him and stabbed him, taking nothing but a watch encrusted with lapis lazuli. The killing involved a single stab wound, and was obviously preplanned, because the killer had picked out a spot between the tennis club parking lot and the club itself that wasn't covered by security cameras and that had a potential access route without being seen.

As she read the files, Maya wasn't so sure about Wendy Poole's death, though. According to the coroner's report, the ruby necklace she wore had been used to strangle her, and then taken. No stab wounds, and the killing had taken place in her own home. To Maya, that all suggested someone with a personal motive, even if the local police hadn't been able to find a family member or friend who didn't have an alibi.

Maya took that case out, too. That left her with Amber, Clarissa, Harvey, Indira Singh, and Tonya Small. Maya kept going.

Of the others, one more didn't seem to fit. Tonya Small's emerald brooch had been stolen, and she had been stabbed, but she'd been stabbed multiple times, and the coroner's report suggested that she'd been dragged, then dumped. That didn't fit the MO of the killer Maya was looking for at all. With Amber, with Clarissa, with Harvey, and with Indira, he'd stabbed them once, then left them where they fell.

Maya looked over Indira's case, and her murder definitely *did* fit the pattern. It was just a few months ago, and she'd had a bracelet taken from her that was set with aquamarines and blue topaz.

Wait…

Now that the other cases were out of the mix, Maya could see another pattern clearly, one that should have been blindingly obvious to her but which had been disguised by the presence of all the other crimes. The victims had had jewelry taken, and there hadn't seemed to be any commonalities in that jewelry, but now, Maya could see at least one obvious one.

They all had blue stones.

The type varied, as did the style of the jewelry, but the blue shine of those jewels and semi-precious stones was a constant. Maya found pictures of the missing pieces in a couple of the files, and the blue shone out at her, obvious, impossible to ignore now that she'd seen it.

Did that get her anywhere, though? Did it make a difference that the killer had a blue stone obsession? The killer could take plenty of other pieces from plenty of other people to complete the set.

Now why had she just thought that? Why was her brain telling her that this was a set? Why that word, when the pieces had so little else in common with one another?

With a start, Maya realized that was the point. The pieces were different. More than that, they were all unique, all handmade or custom built. All designed to be worn on different parts of the body. The killer seemed to be going for a full set of jewels, all taken from people who displayed them openly, all bright, bright blue.

The excitement of that thought was enough to propel Maya up off the bed and out the door. She hammered on Marco's door, and it was less than a minute before he opened it, wearing jeans but no shirt, as if he'd just thrown them on. Maya couldn't help staring for a moment at the muscles revealed beneath, and also couldn't help noticing that Marco had a gun in his hand, ready for trouble.

"Maya, what is it?" For a brief moment, he looked confused and worried, then slightly hopeful, as if he couldn't decide if this was because something dreadful had happened or because Maya had changed her mind about sharing a room.

"I've worked out the connection. The killer is trying to steal a set of blue jewelry!"

Marco seemed slightly taken aback. "That's great, Maya. But is it two a.m. great?"

Maya hadn't realized that was the time. She'd been so caught up in what she was doing that she hadn't noticed.

"Sorry. I just… I think this is something we can go on. We need to talk to the families of the other people who were killed."

"Absolutely," Marco agreed. "Just… in the morning, OK?"

CHAPTER TWENTY TWO

Maya couldn't wait to get going the next morning. It was 8 a.m., so they had sixteen hours left in which to solve this. Sixteen hours in which to find a killer, or a woman would die for Maya's failure.

That thought made her more than eager to talk to the families of the two victims whose cases she hadn't fully explored yesterday. They started with Indira Singh's brother Ravi, who met them at a small house in the suburbs on the edge of the city. He was a smartly dressed man of about thirty, South Asian, with jet black hair and dark eyes. He was wearing a suit, and kept glancing at his watch as Marco and Maya showed up.

"Are we keeping you from something, Mr. Singh?" Maya asked, as he showed them into the home.

"No, it's just that I have people showing up to view this place in about a half hour, so if we could be finished by then?"

"To view?" Maya said, not quite understanding.

"I'm a Realtor. My sister and I worked together."

So this wasn't the family home, but just a place that was for sale. Maya felt a note of frustration at that, because it meant that there weren't going to be any details there that might tell her about Indira's life, no photographs to look at, no objects that she'd carefully collected. It was all down now to what they could get out of Indira's brother. Maya just hoped he was in a position to provide them with something that might prove useful.

"You don't seem concerned that we're looking into your sister's death, Mr. Singh," Marco said.

"I care. I just don't see what good you're going to do," Ravi said, in a challenging tone. "If there were anything to find, the police would have found it by now. And nothing you do will bring Indira back. So I have to spend my time talking to you, when it isn't going to help."

"We already have some leads in this case," Maya said. "We're approaching things from a different angle from the one the police took at the time."

That seemed to pacify Ravi a little. He sighed.

"Look... I want to help. Really. And if you *can* catch whoever did this, I'll do whatever it takes to do that. What do you want to know?"

"Your sister's job must have meant that she met a lot of people," Maya said.

Ravi nodded. "Usually you're showing people around for maybe half an hour, trying to fit in as many viewings a day as possible so that you find that one person who really wants the house. Then there are the clients, of course."

"So someone who wanted to learn about Indira might have been able to pose as someone looking for a viewing in order to get closer to her?" Maya suggested.

"I guess it's possible," Ravi replied. "We do get strange people sometimes. Not just the ones who are obviously just there to look around other people's houses, but sometimes thieves trying to case them to rob, or people coming in because they want to break in later and have some kind of party."

"But those are all about the houses," Marco said. "Did your sister mention anyone paying too much attention to her?"

Maya saw Ravi shrug.

"There are always a few skeevy guys. They see a polished, professional woman and all they see is someone to hit on. Indira was always careful about meeting people. She always made sure that she had their info, and that I knew where she was going, when she was expected back at the office, that kind of thing." Now Maya saw a flash of emotion cross the Realtor's face. "Not that it did any good. All it meant was that I was the one who found her when I went looking after she didn't come back from a viewing."

Maya tried to imagine what that would have been like for him, seeing his sister there like that. She tried to imagine the aftermath, too, when the police would have been questioning him, going through all Indira's friends and contacts. Asking most of the questions she was now.

"My guess is that the police went through most of this with you at the time," she said.

Ravi nodded. "They treated me like a suspect because I was the one who found the body. Thankfully, I was at another viewing."

"It also means that's ground they've gone over before," Maya said. "I want to ask you about something else. Can you tell me about the bracelet your sister wore?"

“The bracelet?” Ravi said, sounding slightly surprised. “I know it was taken, but no one seemed to give it much thought. The police thought that whoever killed her took it just to confuse things and try to make it look like a robbery.”

“We’re exploring other possibilities,” Maya said, “but for that, we need to know more.”

“It… it was a gift from our parents after Indira made her first big sale. Indira was so proud of it, always showing it off. Whenever we had a fight, she’d hold it up like it proved that our parents preferred her.”

He said it almost fondly.

“So people would have seen it?” Marco asked, obviously wanting to establish who might have spotted the bracelet and wanted to kill Indira.

“*Everyone* saw it; that was the point,” Ravi said. “Indira made sure they saw it. She wanted them to see how much she’d succeeded.”

“Thank you,” Maya said. “You’ve been more helpful than you think.”

*

Harvey Jacques didn’t have any family that Maya could find, but she and Marco could at least visit the spot where he’d been killed. They drove over to the tennis club, where they had to stop at a gate, the way barred by a uniformed security guard, a big man whose upright posture and muscled frame had a hint of military as far as Maya could see.

“May I see your passes, please?” he asked.

Maya took out her ID. “I don’t have a pass. I’m here in relation to the death of Harvey Jacques.”

The security guard had a decent poker face, but Maya still caught a flicker of recognition at that name.

“I’m sorry, I think I’m supposed to ask for a warrant if the police want to come onto the site.”

He was apologetic, but in that serious way that professional security had when they weren’t going to budge on an issue.

“We’re looking into a murder,” Marco said.

“I’m aware of that, sir, but I have a job to do here. I have my orders, and I’m going to follow them.”

Maya got out of the car. “Where did you serve?”

She hoped her guess was accurate. Right then, it felt like the only way of getting any information here.

"Afghanistan, then Iraq." There were undercurrents to those words that suggested some of the things that he'd seen in that time.

Maya nodded. "Same. I was in intelligence."

"Marines. Is this all some kind of thing where you try to talk me into letting you in? Because that's not going to happen."

"No, but it tells me that you're the kind of guy who notices things. What's your name?"

"Kent."

"I'm Maya." Maya wasn't sure if this was going to get her everything she needed, but she had to try. "Have you been working here long, Kent?"

"Since before Mr. Jacques was killed, you mean?"

Maya nodded. "I get that you're not allowed to let us in, but I'm also pretty sure that your bosses wouldn't want you to obstruct an inquiry. They don't want the police around because it would attract the wrong kind of attention, but it would also look pretty bad for them if they stop the FBI from finding a killer."

"It shows that you were in intelligence," Kent said. "Always spent their time trying to manipulate people."

Maya shrugged apologetically, even though the comment hurt a little. She found herself thinking of the Moonlight Killer, and the way he tried to control her. She'd also hypothesized from the way he worked that maybe he might have a military background. Maya really didn't like having so much in common with a serial killer.

"Look, I'm not going to apologize for trying to catch the man who killed Harvey Jacques," Maya said. "I'm not trying to manipulate you. I'm just trying to find answers, get the job done."

Being direct seemed like it might work better here. This wasn't a man who was going to respond well to her trying to trick him into giving her answers, but he was also someone who might understand the need to get answers and find a way through this.

"Can you at least answer a few questions about him?" Maya asked. "Anything you're able to tell us might help us to find his killer."

Kent looked like he was considering it. Finally, he nodded. "I guess so. I know that his death cost a lot of the guys here their jobs. A guy gets murdered, and of course the management thinks security messed up. I'm just lucky I wasn't working that day."

"But you saw him around the place other days?" Maya said. "You saw him before he died? You knew who he was?"

Kent the security guard nodded. "I guess. Hard not to. One of those guys who always wanted to be the center of attention, you know?"

Maya knew the type. She'd run into guys like that before.

"Did he *get* that attention?" Maya asked.

"Plenty. I mean, he was this good-looking guy, rich from all his investment stuff, liked to show off that money."

Maya tilted her head to one side. "What did that showing off look like?"

"One of those guys who liked to tip big, especially with the prettier staff members. Liked to buy rounds when he had a good day on the markets. Paid for plenty of tennis lessons. Always flashing that watch of his around."

"That's the watch that was taken from his body?" Maya said, wondering what else the security guard knew.

"That's the one. He always made such a big deal out of it being custom made. My guess is that whoever took it from him did it to shut him up about it."

"We haven't established exactly what happened yet," Marco said, but Maya found herself thinking as Marco kept going. "Did they work out how the guy got in and managed to kill Harvey Jacques without being spotted?"

"Blind spots in the camera coverage," Kent said. "And of course the management doesn't want razor wire on the fences, because it looks bad to the members."

"How did he *know* about the blind spots, though?" Marco asked.

Maya knew the answer to that. "He would have scouted the location beforehand. I bet you and the police spent plenty of time going through the footage, trying to pick out anyone who didn't fit."

"But there were too many people to work through it all," Kent said. "Our guy could have been any one of the members, or the temporary staff, or one of the members' guests."

Too many people to pick out a killer based on the camera footage, but maybe, if they found someone they might be able to look through the footage later to establish if he'd been there.

For now, though, Maya had enough to go with. She didn't want to ask about Harvey's friends and enemies, because Maya was sure at this point that he hadn't been killed by someone for a personal reason, or some problem with his business.

This was about the jewelry. The killer was targeting people who flashed their expensive jewelry around, using it as a way of getting attention, whether that was online, in a club, or in their business life.

The only problem with that new piece of understanding was that it didn't tell Maya *who* the killer was, only what their motivation was.

She and Marco needed something else. She needed a way to work out who the killer was, or at least where he would strike next.

CHAPTER TWENTY THREE

Maya sat in the car, not knowing where to go next.

"Where to?" Marco asked, from the driver's seat.

Maya shook her head.

"Maya?"

"I don't *know*, Marco. I feel like I'm hitting my head against a wall here."

"We're making progress," Marco insisted. "You discovered the linked murders, the fact that the link is the jewelry, the part where the killer is looking for blue stones, the fact that all the victims were people who liked to show off their fancy jewels. It's a lot, Maya."

Maya shrugged. "Not if it doesn't get us anywhere. We know more about why the killer is targeting these victims, but there's nothing to tell us who that killer might be. No DNA hits on a database, no way of picking out an obvious suspect from camera footage, no description, no sense of what he's going to do next."

"We could *try* the camera footage," Marco suggested. "Maybe you'll pick out someone behaving strangely where the local police couldn't."

"I think this guy is good at avoiding cameras," she said. "And it will be a *lot* of hours of footage when we don't know what we're looking for."

"We have to try, Maya. Philadelphia PD will have copies of the footage from Harvey Jacques's case and from the bar. Maybe we can try to see if any faces appear in both sets?"

That was a possibility that caught Maya's attention. After all, before she'd made the link, no one had known that the two cases were connected. There was no reason for anyone to cross-reference the two sets of security footage to see if anything stood out. Maybe there would be a face there. Maybe Maya would actually be able to *see* the killer. With a face, they would be able to check it against DMV records, police files, and FBI databases, so that hopefully it would give them a name and address for the killer.

They drove back toward the police precinct, and the more Maya sat there in the car, forced to do nothing, the more she could feel the time trickling away. She called ahead to Dunlop.

"Agent Gray, got another suspect whose door you're about to kick in?"

Maya was definitely starting to get the impression that Dunlop didn't like her, or maybe it was just that she didn't like the way Maya had complicated the Clarissa Peavey case by bringing in connections to other murders. Maya hoped that wouldn't get in the way of her helping with the footage.

"Nothing like that," Maya said, choosing to treat it as a joke. "But we've had a thought. Because we now believe the Harvey Jacques and Clarissa Peavey murders are linked, would it be possible to go through the camera footage from both the tennis club and the bar to see if any of the same faces appear at both? We wouldn't have to pick out anyone suspicious, it might not even be the same day as the murder if they were there casing the location to work out where the blind spots were."

"That's potentially a lot of footage," Dunlop pointed out.

Maya sighed. "I know, but if it gets us to the killer, it will be worth it."

"If," Dunlop said. "And to go through that amount of footage by hand will take away hours that I could be using to try to question more witnesses and make actual progress on the Peavey case."

Maya had a thought in that regard, though. "We'll run the footage through the FBI's facial recognition software. It should give us an answer pretty quickly, if you can get the files for the footage to me."

This felt more and more like a decent shot at finding an answer the closer they got to the precinct. Maya called Samit next.

"I want to run facial recognition on some security footage," she said. "Do I need to send you the files, or is it something I can do on site?"

"I can send you a copy of the software," Samit said. "But it might be easier if you're prepared to give me access to your system."

They reached the precinct, and Maya headed inside with Marco in her wake and her laptop already open and waiting. She had her phone pressed against her ear, Samit still waiting on the other end of the line. She felt the urgency of it all. She only had hours now before another woman was due to die at the Moonlight Killer's hands. Maya couldn't afford to waste a single second that she might need to actually catch up to whoever they found in the footage.

Dunlop was waiting for her with a flash drive in her hand. "Everything is on here. You really think you can find an answer to this whole thing this way?"

"It has to work," Maya said. The truth was that she didn't have any other ideas. She plugged the flash drive into her computer. "Samit, are you ready?"

"Already on it," the young tech said. "The computer is running through the files now."

Camera footage flashed across Maya's screen, too fast to truly follow. She saw datapoints appear as the computer grabbed information on the faces that appeared.

"It's building up a database on the first set of footage. It should be complete in just a minute," Samit said, as the computer continued to whirl through images in front of Maya. "There. Now, we'll compare the second set of footage to that database, to see if anything matches."

A second set of images, these from the club, started to flicker across the screen as the computer worked on them. More datapoints were scattered across the footage like confetti.

"How's it coming, Samit?" Maya asked, feeling her tension grow. How much longer would it be before she got an answer? How much longer before the computer presented them with a face?

"Finished," Samit said.

"And?"

"No matches."

Those two words felt as if they opened up a yawning pit at Maya's feet, her heart plummeting into it.

"What do you mean?" Maya asked. She knew the answer, but she didn't want to believe it. She had to hear Samit say it.

"None of the faces in the first set of footage match those from the second."

Meaning that the killer hadn't been at both locations. Maybe he'd scouted the bar from outside, or he'd checked out the tennis club in such a way that he hadn't shown up on the cameras.

Did that mean that the two cases weren't connected? No, Maya didn't believe that, *couldn't* believe that. She was sure that these four murders had all been committed by the same person, but the camera footage wasn't there.

They didn't have answers, and that lack felt like an emptiness deep inside Maya. She'd been so hopeful that this might be the breakthrough that she needed, and now… now Maya didn't know what to do next.

She felt as if she couldn't breathe in that moment. She had to step away from Dunlop's desk, backing away, unable to be there right then. She found herself hurrying to the ladies' room, splashing water on her face as she tried to calm down.

It didn't work. She found the image of her sister's face swimming in her mind. Maya didn't have answers, and that meant Megan was in danger. If she didn't find answers in the next few hours, then the Moonlight Killer might take her sister and slip a rope around her neck. He would kill her and then leave her body for Maya to find, the way he'd done with Carmel Johnson.

Even if it wasn't her, even if it was one of his other captives, then a woman would still be dead, and that would be on Maya's conscience, because she would have failed.

There would be repercussions. Maya had played hardball with her boss to get the taskforce that she now headed, all on the basis that the best way to save the women the Moonlight Killer held was to go on solving the cases that he set. That all fell apart if Maya couldn't solve this case. Not only would a woman die tonight, but Harris would go back to trying to raid the Moonlight Killer's supposed location. All the other women he held would die, including Megan.

Just the thought of it all made Maya want to throw up.

She heard a knock at the restroom door.

"Maya, it's me, Marco."

"Go away, Marco. I can't do this. It's not enough time."

"Maya, this isn't you. You're stronger than this."

Maya didn't feel strong in that moment. "Everyone has a breaking point, Marco. This… I've tried everything I can think of. There's no evidence to go on."

"Maya… look, come out of the restroom so we can talk."

Maya didn't want to, but she also knew she couldn't just hide away, couldn't be scared like that. She had to go out and talk to Marco, had to at least face him for this part.

She stepped out of the restroom, and saw Marco standing there, looking worried and sympathetic. That was the last thing Maya needed right then. She didn't need sympathy. She was the one who'd done something wrong, failing to find the killer she'd been sent to locate. If she'd just done better, a woman might be safely released by now. If she'd just—

"Maya, this isn't your fault," Marco said.

"I'm the one investigating this."

"Then *investigate*," Marco said.

"How?" Maya demanded, unable to keep her frustration out of her voice. "I keep coming up with dead ends, and we're running out of time. I don't have any more clues to go on. I don't have any of the answers that I need."

"But you'll find them," Marco said. "You can do this, Maya. You're not just doing this for the victims now, but for all the women who might die in the future. And if anyone can find the answers, it's you."

Maya felt a little calmer with Marco talking her through this, but the problem still remained. "We don't have any evidence, Marco. About the only thing we know when it comes to this guy is that he likes blue jewelry."

"Then how do we use that?" Marco asked her. "Maya, you don't solve cases by grinding down the evidence. You solve them by learning about the killers, understanding them, knowing what they want. Do that now. You know you can."

Maya did her best. She tried to think about the little that she knew about the killer. They knew about his MO, of course, picking out a target and killing them in secluded spots in a way that suggested planning. Maya guessed he might be finding his victims online. There had been plenty of pictures of Amber with her piercing, after all, and Clarissa wasn't the kind of woman who would hold back from posting about her ring the moment she got engaged.

What else? Maya's thoughts kept coming back to the jewelry. All blue, in a way that suggested it meant something to the killer, but what? Was it a reference to someone's eyes, to a jewel he remembered from his past? Was it just his favorite color? It was impossible to know for sure.

Maya tried to think about it another way. What did the killer want? She had the feeling that he wanted to hurt people who showed off what they had too openly, but she also had the feeling that there was more to it than that.

Did it matter that the killer had taken a different type of jewelry each time? Maya had thought before that he might be trying to complete a set of jewelry, but she'd gotten distracted by the need to try to find more. Maybe this was the best clue she was going to get. Maybe if she could work out what the killer would still need, it might let her catch up to him as she went to take it.

Except that there was no guarantee that the killer would strike again anytime soon. The killings had been spaced out, months apart, so why wouldn't there be another gap like that now? That would put them well past the deadline the Moonlight Killer had set.

Why had he set that deadline, though? Maya had thought that it was just cruelty on his part, but now another possibility occurred to her: that he knew something she didn't. He had to know that the only way to get to the killer was to catch him as he tried to strike again, so he had to have a reason to think that the killer was going to do so before tonight.

Now, Maya just had to work out what that reason was.

CHAPTER TWENTY FOUR

It was time for Frank to make another call, deep in his bunker that night. If that call went well, then tonight, he would travel to collect his newest bunny.

A big part of that was the phone call he made next, to the burner phone he'd sent Lee Gibbons. As with the last time the two had spoken, Frank made very sure that his voice scrambler was running before he hit the button to call it.

"Are you in position?" he asked Lee, as soon as the other man picked up.

"I'm looking at the house now," his contact replied. He didn't sound entirely enthusiastic about it, but that was what one got when one had to rely on blackmail.

"And?" Frank said. "I take it that you've found a way in?"

"Listen," Lee said. "If I do this, we're square, right? No more little phone calls? No other jobs like this coming out of nowhere?"

There was always a stage where they tried to show their defiance. For dear Maya, it had been the attempts by the FBI to find him in spite of his instructions not to do so. For Lee, it seemed to be this.

"You need to focus on what will happen if you *don't* do this right, Lee," Frank said. "Tell me about the house."

There was a pause, presumably as Lee remembered his situation.

"Pretty standard," Lee said, with an obvious note of resentment. "There's an alarm on the side. Pretty standard model. Cutting the wires should deal with it. Best way in is through the garage, but there's no approach to that from the front. Too open. That means going in through the yard. No dogs that I've spotted. There's a side passage that will lead around to it. Shouldn't be a problem."

He sounded confident about it. Too confident? That was another problem with working with other people: Frank found himself second-guessing them, trying to work out if they were actually right when they promised that they were. Trying to work out if they were actually competent.

That was why it was vital to select the right people for the job, as he'd done with Maya. He'd seen a need to have cold cases investigated, he'd seen a brilliant investigator, and the connection hadn't been hard to make. Of course, it helped that she fit into his plans in other ways, too.

Frank reminded himself that Lee was exactly the right person in this case. He was a successful burglar, and that meant that he could assess this situation as well as anyone.

"And the location of the target?"

"She's asleep," Lee said, sounding confident. "Bedroom at the back of the house."

"Where is the bed in that room?" Frank asked.

"Left side as you enter the door."

"Any obstacles in the way?"

"No."

Lee had that casual confidence again. A part of Frank wanted to go there and make sure of this himself, sitting outside the house until he was sure, but he had his bunnies to think of.

Honestly, there were days when he wondered if all of this was worth it, if it might not be simpler just to kill all of them and move on. If he did that, though, then the confusion would still be out there. The murders by pretenders would still be seen as his, and there would be no way for people to see the beauty of his full design.

No, he had to act, and he had to do it now.

"Are you still there?" Lee asked.

"Yes," Frank said, realizing that he'd been lost in his thoughts for several seconds. "I was considering the situation. Very well, I will proceed. I will travel there shortly."

He hung up, not bothering to say goodbye. He pulled on his mask and gloves, then headed out into the main body of the bunker.

"Lights out, bunnies!" he called. "Time for you to go back to your hutches!"

They hurried to do it, moving with the speed of the frightened. They went into their cages, and Frank went to lock them inside, one by one. As he did so, he looked over each of the cages carefully, trying to make sure that none of them had smuggled anything into their hutches that they might use to hurt themselves.

He wasn't a man who repeated his mistakes. He didn't allow room for problems to arise.

"Sleep tight, my bunnies," he said, once they were all firmly inside. "When you wake, you'll have a new little friend to join you."

*

Frank drove, not pausing. He wanted to be away from his bunnies for as little time as possible to allow the minimum amount of space for something to go wrong. It took slightly more than two hours before his dark, unremarkable van pulled up on the street that held Claire Rainford's home.

He turned it off and sat there, making sure there was no reaction from the surrounding neighborhood. At this time of the night, though, the whole suburb was quiet and dark. If anyone had woken at the sound of the van, they would quickly go back to sleep.

Even so, Frank looked around carefully, wanting to make sure that there would be no police waiting for him. He checked a police scanner, too. There was no chatter that might indicate that he was walking into some kind of trap. No indication that Lee had tried anything stupid like trying to betray him.

Finally, Frank was satisfied. He got everything he would need tonight, the restraints, the sedative, and then he slipped out of the van, pulling a hat down over his face so his features wouldn't be too obvious if someone happened to look out. He wasn't wearing a mask yet, because that would only induce someone to call the police if they saw it. A man in a hat might be out walking. One in a mask was obviously there to rob someone.

Walking briskly along the street, he looked around for the side passage Lee had mentioned, and found it in under a minute.

Frank started to make his way down it on nearly silent feet, then froze in place as he spotted a figure ahead, hiding in the shadows near the back of the house. Was this an ambush? An attempt to capture or kill him?

Frank was armed, of course. He had a sharp knife at his belt, and a gun in a concealed carry holster. Not that he wanted to use either of them. It wasn't a full moon, and that mattered to Frank. His work required deaths, but only when the rules allowed for them, or when others had broken his rules.

Then he heard Lee's voice.

"Is that you?" the thief called out, stepping forward. "The guy from the phone?"

Too late, Frank realized that he should have put a mask on for this part. He hadn't wanted to do so until he was in the house, because he'd wanted to be able to pass off his presence as something else if he were seen, yet now, he found himself instantly regretting it.

Especially since it was now clear that Lee could see him.

"Lee?" Frank said. "What are you doing here?"

Frank fingered his knife as he said the words.

"I thought that was what you *wanted.* I thought that's what you blackmailed me for."

Frank took a step forward, out into the passage behind the house. "I got you involved to *scout* this place for me, not to be part of a break-in. You aren't supposed to be here."

This wasn't what he'd planned, and Frank didn't like it when things didn't go according to plan. He prepared contingencies ahead of operations precisely to prevent this kind of thing from happening, yet with the urgent need to replace his lost bunny, with the need to watch over the others, there had been no time to plan for every possibility in all this.

Frank knew what he had to do. The man in front of him had to die. He'd seen Frank's face. He could connect him to the disappearance that was about to happen, yet the necessity of it filled Frank with turmoil. He wasn't a man who stabbed people at random. He killed with a purpose. He strangled them when he killed them. This wasn't what he did. It was out of control, and Frank valued control almost more than anything. The conflict between the two made his temples throb with tension.

He could delay the decision, at least.

"Since you're here, you might as well make yourself useful," Frank said. An extra pair of hands might be helpful in getting closer to Claire Rainford. And Frank was more than happy to leave Lee's body in Claire's house, where it wouldn't be found for a day or two.

"What does that mean?"

"It means that you're going to help me to do this. You're going to take care of the alarm."

They headed over the fence together, landing lightly in the yard of the house. Frank padded forward on silent feet. As soon as Lee dealt with the alarm and got them inside, Frank would cut his throat. Quick and silent, just the way he'd trained to do it.

He drew the knife in readiness, holding it close to his leg so that his dark pants would hide the shine. A few more strides and they would be at the alarm box.

Light flooded the yard, painfully bright in its intensity. Frank was almost blind from it for the seconds that followed, and in that blindness, a woman's voice called out.

"I'm calling the cops! You'd better get out of here!"

This was why Frank didn't like leaving things to other people. He'd assumed that Lee would be competent at his job, but the man had missed something as simple as a motion sensor. Incompetent, stupid.

As the spots started to fade from his eyes, Frank saw Lee turning to run. No, he didn't get to leave this place. He didn't get to mess up Frank's plans and then just flee into the night like nothing had happened.

Frank slashed out with the knife, aiming low on impulse. He hacked across the back of Lee's legs, slicing the hamstrings. Frank heard the other man scream and saw him topple like an animal brought down by a tripwire.

Frank moved in, ready to finish him off.

"I've got a gun!" the woman called out, and then a shot rang out, far too close to Frank for comfort. Another thing that his supposed expert had missed.

Now it was Frank's turn to run, heading for the fence, back the way he'd come, zigzagging so that he wouldn't present a good target.

He leapt the fence in one smooth movement, clambering over it and sprinting down the side passage. Already in the distance, he thought that he could hear sirens. It was vital that he made it to his van in time.

Frank ran to it and all but leapt inside, starting the engine with a kind of panic that he simply didn't feel normally. He drove off, taking the first couple of streets at speed. At that point, Frank had to force himself to slow down, to drive within the speed limit, to not draw attention. It was the right move. Frank saw a police car drive past, lights flashing. He resisted the urge to duck down as it did so, and he kept an eye on it in the rearview mirror. It didn't spin around.

Frank was furious as he started his drive back, taking a circuitous route to make sure he wasn't being followed. Utterly furious at Lee, but also at himself. He'd chosen a fool to work with on this, and now that fool was back there, having seen Frank's face.

Worse still, the abduction was a failure. He didn't have a new bunny to replace his lost one.

CHAPTER TWENTY FIVE

Maya sat in front of her laptop, trying to work out what the Moonlight Killer had seen that she hadn't. There had to be something. The deadline he'd given had to mean something or what was the point of it?

Was anyone going to be in Philadelphia who otherwise wouldn't? Someone who showed off their jewels too much online? Maya could think of a dozen ways that might happen, from rappers to minor celebrities, visiting businesspeople to airline cabin crew.

That was a lot of people to check through, trying to find the ones who were showing off the kind of jewelry the killer wanted. How was Maya even supposed to find them?

The answer to that was obvious enough: the same way the killer was presumably finding his victims. She needed to go through social media, looking for someone who fit the description, someone who would catch his attention.

"OK," she said to Marco and Detective Dunlop. "We need to look for people who might be the killer's next victim."

"And what makes you think he's going to kill again so soon?" Dunlop asked.

Maya realized she wasn't going to be able to explain it to the detective's satisfaction without giving away everything about the situation with the hostages and the Moonlight Killer. That would make things worse, not better, and Maya was determined to avoid it.

"You just need to trust me," she said.

"I don't need to do anything," Detective Dunlop replied. "You've already gotten me to waste more time than I should on this business with the camera footage."

"Maya saved you hours of work on that," Marco shot back. "And it didn't pan out. So what? Have you never had a lead that didn't pan out, Detective?"

"Plenty, but that's all I seem to be getting from the two of you right now," Dunlop said. "I'm going to put some actual work in on my own case. If the two of you want to start looking for *more* possible murders, that's your business, but don't do it at my desk."

Maya realized then that they weren't going to get any more help from the detective, and possibly not from the Philadelphia PD as a whole. That was a pity, but for this, she suspected that they already had all the resources they needed.

"Come on, Marco," she said. "We don't have a lot of time to lose."

The two of them headed out of the precinct and back to the car. Marco drove them clear of the department and then picked a spot to park in, so that they could start the work of trying to find a likely victim.

"What's the real reason you think there will be another victim tonight?" Marco asked.

"The deadline," Maya said. "We've had cases before where the deadline has been about someone else being in danger, and with one so short, there has to be a reason for it."

Marco considered that. "It's possible. Of course, it's also possible that the Moonlight Killer just wants you to fail."

Maya nodded. "I thought that earlier. But that's the thing. He *doesn't* want me to fail. Me succeeding and clearing his name in these cases matters to him enough that he's kidnapped thirteen women so far and built or acquired some kind of underground bunker. This matters to him. He's not going to mess up one of the cases by giving me too little time in which to solve it."

"That presupposes that he's behaving rationally," Marco pointed out.

"He is," Maya insisted. "All of this makes sense to him. Yes, in some way that we don't understand, but it makes sense to *him*. He's been about rules and patterns so far, and he wouldn't just deliberately cheat in his own game."

Maya paused for a moment, and then said the other part of it.

"I have to believe this, Marco, because the alternative is that a woman is going to die and there's nothing I can do to save her. This has to be about another murder happening tonight. It *has* to be."

"All right," Marco said. He got out his phone. "What exactly are we looking for?"

"Anyone who might fit the victim profile, so anyone who is flashing around some piece of blue jewelry. My guess is not a watch, ring, piercing, or bracelet. I think the killer is trying to complete a set here."

"If it *is* a set, then he's missing a necklace for a centerpiece," Marco said.

Maya could only agree. Yes, there were brooches and tiepins, hairpins and jeweled handbags, but a set of jewelry without some kind of necklace seemed incomplete, somehow.

"I'll check social media," Marco said.

"And I'll get on to Samit. This kind of large-scale search for information is going to take all three of us."

Maya called Samit. If he was getting exasperated with how often she was calling for his help, he didn't show any sign of it. Maybe he was just glad that he got to play a part in all of this.

"Samit, I'm trying to find a possible next victim for our killer. That means anyone in the Philadelphia area who is showing off with a lot of jewelry featuring blue precious or semi-precious stones. We think it's most likely to be a necklace, but just so long as it isn't a bracelet, piercing, watch, or ring."

"That's going to be a lot of potential results," Samit warned her.

"Let's check, then we can work out what the most likely one is after we have something to work with," Maya replied. Of course there were going to be plenty of people on Instagram or TikTok who had elaborate jewelry and wanted to show it off. If they could at least get some possibilities, then they could perhaps begin to narrow it all down.

Maya set to work, using her laptop to search for anyone who might fit the victim profile. She tried to think the way the killer might as he selected his victim. He would be looking for the jewelry first, and he was only interested in blue stones for reasons that only really made sense to him, so Maya started using words like "sapphire" and "jewelry" as search terms in social media.

As Samit had predicted, the problem wasn't finding results. The problem was the sheer number of hits Maya got with each term. It was overwhelming, and certainly didn't give her a single clear result. The search terms felt far too general, taking in too many things that clearly didn't fit the pattern of the serial killer she was hunting.

There were pictures of everything from pieces of jewelry people had made to them showing off some new acquisition. Maya looked for a way to discount the former and focus on the latter, because she didn't believe that the killer was going after the makers of jewelry. It mattered at least as much to him that these were people who showed off, who rubbed the wealth and the status that the jewelry represented in people's faces.

Maya needed to find those people, and if the internet didn't have quite so many of them, then it would be a lot easier for her right then. She found herself scrolling through, imagining that she was the killer, trying to work out what would catch her eye if she were.

No, that was no good. There were too many flashy pieces of jewelry and certainly no way of going around to every possible owner to try to find out if they'd seen anyone suspicious near them. Maya needed to think of something else.

Maya was still thinking about it when Samit called back.

"Agent Gray, I think I might have something. I'm sending a link to your inbox."

Maya found the link and clicked on it. She found herself staring at an advertisement for a charity fundraiser at the Philadelphia Museum of Antiquities. The theme of it was simple: a night in which the guests would be able to wear pieces from the museum's extensive collection of rare and ancient jewelry. The centerpiece of it all was a large sapphire necklace, which glittered such a clear blue that Maya knew as soon as she saw it that the killer wouldn't be able to look away from it.

He wouldn't be able to resist the temptation of the event, either. A night where the whole purpose was for the people who went there to show off their wealth and taste while wearing expensive jewelry? It promised *exactly* the kind of victim he'd gone after before, and more.

Then there was the date. The gala was tonight. *This* was the reason that the deadline was at midnight. Either Maya would have found the killer by then or they would have claimed another victim, taking the necklace as they went.

"Samit," Maya said. "I need you to get the museum on the phone right now. I need you to get me and Marco in there, and I need to be the one with the sapphire necklace."

"I'll get on it. What if they refuse?"

"They won't refuse. The alternative is that a killer goes into their event and kills one of their patrons in front of everybody else. I can't imagine that will be good for their fundraiser."

"OK, I'll call them now," Samit said, and hung up.

Maya could see Marco looking across at her.

"What was all that about?" he asked.

“The Philadelphia Museum of Antiquities is holding a gala night where patrons get to wear some of the pieces on display in the collection. The killer is going to be there. I can feel it.”

Maya turned the computer toward him, so that Marco could see it.

“He’s going to go after whoever wears this,” Maya said. “It’s obvious.”

“And when you just said to Samit that the sapphire was yours?” Marco asked, sounding suddenly very worried.

“I plan to be the one wearing it,” Maya said.

“Maya, no, you can’t!”

“It’s the best move,” Maya insisted. “If I let one of the patrons wear that necklace, then I put them in danger. Even if I follow them closely, there’s no guarantee that the killer won’t find a moment when they’re alone, and if the killer sees us following them, then they might just decide to bail on the evening. This way, the killer comes to me.”

“To try to kill you,” Marco said. “Do you have any idea how dangerous this could be?”

He sounded scared for Maya, but Maya wasn’t going to stop just because of that. She certainly wasn’t about to let Marco tell her that she couldn’t go.

“It’s a lot safer than things will be for my sister if we don’t catch this guy,” Maya replied.

“You can’t just make yourself into bait for a killer.” Marco was looking less happy about this by the second. “What if he hurts you? What if he kills you?”

The concern there might just have been the concern of one partner for another, but to Maya, it felt like more than that, and the strength of it touched her, made her wonder just how close she was getting with Marco.

At the same time, though, she had to do this.

“Marco, it’s already being arranged,” she said. “Samit is on the phone with the museum as we speak. And the killer won’t have a chance to kill me. You’ll be right there, and I’m more than capable of protecting myself even if things go wrong.”

She could see that Marco was still uncomfortable about this.

“It’s the best way, Marco, the *only* way. We’ll lure the killer in, and when he tries to strike, we’ll be waiting for him.”

“All right,” Marco said. “I don’t like it, but all right. There’s just one more problem, though.”

“What’s that?”

“Where do you think you’re going to get a suitable dress for the gala at this kind of notice?”

CHAPTER TWENTY SIX

Justin pulled on his suit carefully, precisely, wanting to look as neat as possible for tonight. He adjusted his bow tie in the mirror, and he had to admit that he admired himself a little as he did so.

From his chiseled physique and perfect blond hair to the steady, determined gaze of the blue eyes beneath, he'd built himself into something a long way from the fat, scared little kid he'd been. He'd become successful, respected, liked by his colleagues at the software firm where he worked. People thought he was kind and good, terms that had never been used when he was growing up.

Yet some things stayed with you, no matter how hard you tried to run from them. Justin knew that better than anyone.

He adjusted the charm bracelet he wore on one wrist, blue stones flashing. There was the piercing he'd taken from Amber Kaley, the ring from Clarissa Peavey. He wore the watch he'd taken from Harvey Jacques on that wrist just below it, and the bracelet from Indira Singh just above. All of them were reminders of what he did, what he *had* to do.

He was sure his grandmother would disagree, if she were still alive. Her earrings dangled from the bracelet with the rest, although Justin's biggest regret was that a heart attack had claimed her before the scared kid he'd been could pluck up the courage to do it.

If she were here, she would stand over him as she had so many times before, calling him stupid or lazy, lashing out with hands laden with costume jewelry. Justin could still feel the pain of the blows she'd landed with the rings she wore, so heavy and encrusted with fake gems that she might as well have been wearing knuckle dusters.

"It's your fault your parents died!" she yelled at him whenever she wanted to hurt him even worse than the blows could. "I don't know why I took you in!"

She always said it like it was some great benediction that she'd bestowed, rather than dragging Justin into a living hell of abuse. Like it hadn't been far better for him in the foster home for the couple of years after she'd died. Like the blue stones of the earrings on his wrist didn't haunt his dreams.

The earrings had been the only things of hers he'd kept. The rest of it had been sold: the house, the car, all of it. The costume jewelry hadn't fetched much, even though his grandmother had worn it like the pieces were the most precious things in the world. She'd shown it off like a peacock displaying its plumage, flashing it around as she wandered through her social circle, pretending that she was important.

Worse, people *liked* her for it. Justin could remember his grandmother's friends only too well. She'd been the life and soul of the party. None of them had seen, or wanted to see, the things she did when they weren't around.

For a while, Justin had thought that he was over all of it. Or at least, he'd thought he'd had it under control. He could deal with the nightmares, deal with all the ways his upbringing had cut him off from people.

Then he'd started to see the people who were just like his grandmother. He'd seen them flashing their jewelry around, seen that deep blue that was the same as her earrings, and he'd known that they were just like his grandmother. The more he looked at them, the more he saw the ways that they pretended to be good, tried too hard, demanded attention.

He knew, as certainly as he knew his own name, that somewhere in their lives there would be someone who was suffering the way he had suffered.

So he'd killed them.

It was simpler than he'd thought it would be at the start. Justin had been half convinced that he wouldn't be able to do it, but it had turned out that it was easy. Once he was in front of them, all he saw was his grandmother standing there. One thrust of a knife in the right place was all it took to end them. The only hard part of it was the planning, finding the time and the place where that one thrust would be able to do its work.

He'd done it, though. Every time, he'd done it.

Yet still he kept finding people like them, and slowly, he'd started to build up a set of jewelry that was more than a match for anything his grandmother wore. He hadn't thought of it as a set, but now… *now* Justin needed to complete that set the way he needed air or water.

When he'd seen the advertisements for the gala tonight, Justin had known instantly that it was something he would have to attend. He couldn't be anywhere else tonight and sleep comfortably.

A place where people were going *specifically* to wear the most expensive jewelry and flash it around? It was a sinkhole of epic proportions, a boil that needed to be lanced. It was an opportunity to send a message, to tell the world that some people's actions wouldn't be tolerated.

That was why Justin had a fine evening suit on now. That was why he'd paid an exorbitant amount of money for a ticket. That was why he'd spent time going through public records, learning as much as he could about the museum's layout, looking for the perfect spot.

He'd planned all of this for so long, and this would be the culmination of his work. Tonight, he would take the blue necklace, and the person wearing it would die. His message would be sent, his collection complete.

Tonight, everything he'd worked so hard toward for so long would finally be finished.

CHAPTER TWENTY SEVEN

This had to be one of the stranger operations Maya had undertaken in her career. She was at home bursting into buildings or undertaking surveillance, working through the evidence of a murder or chasing after a suspect.

Going dress hunting in preparation for a sting operation was something Maya wasn't used to.

She was currently standing in the changing rooms of a particularly fancy clothing rental store, trying to find something that fit her properly, looked good, *and* could give her decent access to her Glock without the sidearm's presence being too obvious.

Maya tried a slinky black dress, but it was too tight. If it came to a chase, she wouldn't be able to keep up with a suspect. A deep burgundy dress was far too long and billowing, so that it would only tangle Maya if she needed to act quickly.

Maya decided to work it all out from first principles. Deal with the practical first, and the rest would fall into place. She hoped. She and Marco only had an hour or so now before the gala was due to start. What did she need tonight?

Weapon access was crucial. Could she keep her Glock in a purse? Possible, but Maya didn't like the time it might take to open a purse and start to go through it to get to a weapon. Maya had too much experience of trying to find *anything* she wanted in a purse to trust something life or death to it.

No, she wanted the weapon holstered on her. In a dress, probably the best way to do that was a thigh holster. To access that, though…

Maya's eyes fell on a purple dress so dark it was almost black, slit high up the side. Maya slipped her pistol into her thigh holster and tried on the dress. It fit her beautifully, giving the suggestion of being low cut without actually exposing much. It flowed around her legs as she tried to move, and crucially, there was no glimpse of the Glock as she did so. Maya let down her hair so that it spilled loose over her shoulders, allowing it to hide an earpiece with a link back to Samit.

Yes, she thought that might work. The only question now was shoes. She was pretty sure that her usual work shoes would be a dead giveaway that she wasn't really supposed to be there, but were heels really a good idea if she might have to chase someone?

Maya guessed that she could always kick them off if she had to, and added a pair to the ensemble. She took the time to adjust her makeup to the outfit, going for more than she normally wore, adding in eyeshadow and lipstick in a dark plum that worked well with the purplish tinge of the dress. She picked up one of the purses that were lying around the changing room waiting for her to make a selection. It was a simple silver shoulder strap purse, small, but more than big enough for Maya to put a pair of cuffs in for when she needed them.

Her outfit complete, she stepped out, feeling far more self-conscious than she'd thought she would at the thought of looking like this in front of Marco.

He was out there in the front of the rental place, resplendent in a tuxedo that followed the contours of his swimmer's body, only serving to accentuate how good-looking he was. He came over to stand in front of Maya, staring at her.

"Wow," he said, the word seeming to come out almost unconsciously. "You... you're... you clean up pretty well, Agent Gray."

"You don't look so bad yourself," Maya replied. His hair was neater than usual, his boyish good looks only highlighted by the formality of his clothing.

In that moment, it was impossible to look away from Marco. It was as if there was a connection between the two of them that was greater than just the fact that he looked so good; it was as if Maya were seeing him in some new way, some deeper way.

Maya found herself leaning closer to him, wanting nothing more right then than to move in and kiss him. She was as attracted to him in that moment as she ever had been, if not more.

Unfortunately, or perhaps thankfully, the sales clerk chose that moment to cough politely.

It was enough to break the spell between them, bringing Maya back to herself enough to take a step back. She saw Marco doing the same. The two of them needed to keep their heads clear tonight. They had to remember that they weren't going to a party; they were setting out to catch a killer.

“I trust everything is to your satisfaction?” the clerk said.

“Everything is perfect,” Maya said. At least, it was until the clerk rang up the cost of the rental for the evening. She found herself grateful in that moment that she would be able to put all of this in as expenses.

She hoped so, at least.

She and Marco headed out to the car, before driving over in the direction of the museum of antiquities. While they drove, Maya made a call to Detective Tanner. She went with Tanner rather than Dunlop because she was pretty certain that Dunlop wasn’t going to be taking her calls right then.

Tanner answered quickly enough, although his tone made it clear that he was wary.

“What do you want, Agent Gray?”

“What makes you think I’m not just calling to exchange info on my case?” Maya asked.

“Maybe because I had a conversation with Detective Dunlop in which she spent most of it complaining about you. What do you want, Agent?”

Maya sighed. “Marco and I have found a place we believe the killer in the Amber Kaley case is going to be tonight.”

There was silence on Detective Tanner’s end of the line for a few seconds. He was obviously thinking about all the things Dunlop must have told him, but at the same time, Maya guessed that he wasn’t going to pass up a chance to catch the killer.

“You’re serious?” he said.

“It’s not something I would joke about.” This was something Maya was deadly serious about. Lives were at stake in this. The gala would go on until midnight, which meant that if she and Marco failed to find the killer there, they would have failed completely. A woman would die at the Moonlight Killer’s hands.

Just the thought of that made her sick with worry.

“Where?” Tanner asked.

“There’s a gala tonight at the museum of antiquities,” Maya explained. “I believe that our killer is going after people who show off fancy jewelry, and a… source suggests that he is planning to strike again before the end of tonight. That combination says that the gala is the target, and I believe that I know which piece of jewelry he’s going after.”

There was another brief pause on the other end of the line. "That's not a lot of solid evidence."

"It's also the best chance we have," Maya said.

"What I'm saying is that if you're asking for a bunch of extra cops on the place, I'm not going to be able to swing the overtime," Detective Tanner said.

Maya was disappointed. She'd felt sure that Tanner would be willing to help even if Dunlop wasn't.

"But there will be some police around there anyway, just with the scale of the event," Tanner said. "And if you're sure about this, then I guess I can swing by too. I'll bring Dunlop. She might not like the way you've complicated her case, but she wants answers in this as badly as anyone does."

It wasn't much, but Maya figured it was better than nothing. Besides, maybe a massively increased police presence wouldn't help in a situation like this. There was always a chance that it would scare off the killer, and Maya couldn't afford to do that. She needed to catch him tonight.

They were approaching the museum now. They parked and then headed for the doors, where a security guard stepped into their path.

"I'm sorry, but the gala does not begin for another half hour, so unless you're one of the patrons getting ready for the event…"

Maya flashed her ID, grateful that the guard had mistaken the two of them for ordinary guests. It meant that their disguises were working, and that there was a chance they might be able to fool the killer when he arrived.

"Agent Gray, FBI. We called ahead."

"Ah, yes," the guard said. "We were told to expect you. Go through. Ground floor. You want Professor Allison. He shouldn't be hard to spot."

Maya went through with Marco, feeling more like a secret agent in that moment than she had in all the rest of her job put together. She walked through onto the main floor, where glass cases containing exhibits were spread out all around. There were artifacts that looked as though they'd been taken from all over the world, from African statuary to Egyptian funeral masks to a collection of antique Japanese swords. A mezzanine level sat above, no doubt filled with more items.

For today, though, it seemed that many of the cases had been rearranged to make sure that items of jewelry were in some of the most prominent locations. Maya could already see a few patrons wandering among them, some of them already wearing artifacts as if they were simple items of costumery rather than precious antiquities. Maya saw a fat man wearing a golden torc that had to be Viking or Celtic, a young woman in a cocktail dress wearing a small topaz pendant whose chain seemed to be made in the shapes of animals of the Chinese zodiac, a wealthy dowager wearing a series of bracelets that ran up both her arms almost as far as her elbow-length gloves, and at least a dozen others.

She found that the security guard was right; it wasn't hard to spot Professor Allison, because he was the one looking panicked at the heart of all the last-minute preparations for the event.

He was a man in his fifties, bald and bespectacled, looking uncomfortable in his tuxedo and bow tie as he gestured to someone up above.

"No, that's still not right, Gwen. We need to get those lights fixed or the exhibits just won't sparkle properly!"

"Professor Allison?" Maya said, approaching him.

He turned to her and Maya had her ID ready, holding it as discreetly as she could so that only he would see. She didn't think the killer would be in the room yet, but she also didn't want to take any more chances than she had to, not now.

"Ah, yes, of course," the professor said, although the look of worry on his face only seemed to increase. "While the museum is happy to offer the FBI every assistance in this matter, I hope that you will *please* be discreet. This event took months to set up, and I would hate for it to be ruined by any… commotion."

Maya wanted to point out that a little trouble was probably far better than the professor seeing one of his guests murdered, but she knew that wouldn't help to make him any more cooperative.

"We'll do our best," she said instead. She gestured to herself and Marco. "That's why we're doing it this way. Now, we just need the necklace."

"Yes, yes, of course," the professor said, although he didn't sound entirely comfortable. "If you'll follow me, I'll take you to it."

He led the way to one of the cases, and as Maya stood in front of it, she could almost, *almost* understand the killer's obsession. She'd seen pictures of the sapphire necklace, of course, but it was very different seeing it in real life. The stone seemed larger, somehow, in a platinum setting with a chain of broad links.

Maya waited while Professor Allison unlocked the case and reverentially lifted it from within.

"The stone in this necklace was found in India in 1700," the professor explained as he lifted it. "It was smuggled out, and found its way into the hands of a Spanish merchant, who set it into the chain, thinking to make a gift of it to the then king of Spain. His ship ran into pirates, though, and the necklace disappeared for almost two hundred years before being acquired by a wealthy Philadelphia businessman. It was in his family until a generation ago, when a lack of heirs led to the dissolution of his estate. One of our patrons acquired the piece, and put it with us on permanent loan."

He held it out as if he might put it around Maya's neck, but Marco took it from him.

"Let me."

He moved close to Maya, clipping it in place around her neck, the stone hanging down to sit brightly against the purple black of her dress.

"You look perfect," Marco said.

Maya couldn't help smiling back at him. "Let's hope that the killer feels the same way."

Everything was set. The gala would be starting soon. Now, Maya just had to wait for Amber Kaley's killer to come to her.

CHAPTER TWENTY EIGHT

Maya had to admit that the gala was impressive. The museum had quickly filled up with people moving among the exhibits, glasses of champagne in their hands. Maya took a glass of orange juice instead, needing to keep a clear head for this.

There were more wealthy people there in that one place than Maya had seen together before. She was sure she recognized a couple of them, although she couldn't remember from where. She guessed that it probably wasn't from the FBI's most wanted list, but simply because they were sufficiently famous that it had gotten through even to her.

"That necklace is fabulous," an older man in a white tuxedo said, and Maya had to resist the natural instinct to tense up, ready for danger. She was pretty sure this wasn't their killer, just as the last three people to offer compliments on the jewelry hadn't been.

"Thank you," Maya said.

"How did you get to be the lucky one to wear that piece?" the man asked.

Maya spread her hands. "Just fortunate, I guess."

"I wish I had that kind of fortune. What line of business are you in to afford to be one of the museum's biggest patrons?"

"Doing this tonight was a gift from a friend," Maya said, not caring that the people who heard that probably assumed she was the lover of some rich man. It was a lot easier than trying to answer questions about some area of business that she knew nothing about. "Excuse me, I should keep mingling."

It was important to keep moving, so that Maya could try to work her way through as much of the room as possible. She felt sure the killer would be here somewhere now, so Maya wanted to look at everyone there, see who was watching her too closely, who was behaving strangely.

The problem was that a lot of people were looking her way, enough that Maya had to resist the urge to blush at being the center of attention. She was sure a lot of it was just down to her wearing the most expensive jewel in the room, but at least a part of her wanted to believe it had something to do with the dress and the makeup.

Maya spotted Marco. He was working the room nearby, keeping a careful eye on her from a distance, while glancing around, obviously trying to spot any sign of the killer before he made his move.

Maya went over to one of the exhibits: a display devoted to the process of the jeweler's art in the sixteenth century. The actual reason for looking at it, though, was so Maya could use the reflections in the glass case to look for anyone watching her who might try to act more normally when she was looking their way.

It didn't help that the room's lighting was dimmed, multicolored spotlights picking out every facet of the jewels there. Classical music filled the air: Bach and Brahms played by a quartet in the corner. Under other circumstances, it would have been beautiful, but when Maya was trying to find a killer, it was simply distracting.

Maya was only too aware of the time ticking by. The gala was in full swing by now, and it was getting closer to midnight, little by little. Maya felt tension thrumming through her at that thought, and at the thought of what would happen if the killer didn't make a move before the time came. What if he waited until after the gala and struck as people were coming out?

No, Maya was certain that it wouldn't work like that. It couldn't. If the killer wanted the necklace, then he had to strike while she was here, before it was locked away again, away from his grasp.

The thought of the killer somewhere in the room with Maya only served to increase that tension. Every time someone came near her, Maya found herself tensing, ready to protect herself if a knife came toward her. Yet there were so many people pressed so close that it was almost impossible to keep track of all of them.

That was a terrifying thought, when the killer's MO was to step in and stab before the victim had a clue what was happening. Maya was betting her life on being able to spot him before he made that strike, being able to stop him in time.

Maya wondered why no one was trying to get her alone. She knew the killer wouldn't just strike on the open floor, but she'd assumed that she would have to be in the busiest space for him to have the best possible chance to spot her.

Now, though, Maya suspected that wasn't cutting it. The only way Maya was going to lure him in was if she found a way to make herself a more attractive target.

"That's a really lovely necklace," a woman said, approaching.

"Thank you," Maya replied. "Excuse me, I think I need to go get some air."

Obviously, no one was allowed to just wander outside, particularly not while wearing the museum's precious jewels. The patrons might be allowed to wear them tonight, but the museum was doing everything it could to keep the jewels secure in spite of that.

Maya went upstairs instead. There were fewer people here, most of the patrons wanting to be on the ground floor where everyone could see them. Maya took a slow walk around the mezzanine, pretending to look at some of the display cases and paintings that lined the walls. She saw Marco coming up the stairs behind her, obviously having waited briefly before following, so that it wouldn't be obvious that he was there to protect her.

Still, Maya wasn't isolated enough. She looked around at the museum's cameras, trying to work out what they covered and what they didn't. There were balconies beyond the mezzanine level, and as far as Maya could see, the cameras didn't cover those. Trying to pick one that could be approached as far from any of the cameras as possible, Maya slipped out into the cool of the night air.

She waited out there, sipping her orange juice and leaning back against the railing, pretending to enjoy the party from a distance. That was important, because she didn't want to have her back to the gala when a killer might be coming out of it at any moment to target her.

Still, no one came. Maya stood there for several minutes, and by now, she thought that the killer would have taken his chance. It took her another few moments to realize the problem: Marco was hovering too close to the door to the balcony. It meant that anyone who came out to her would have to go straight past him, close enough that he would obviously recognize them afterwards.

Maya touched her hand to her earpiece, as innocuously as she could. "Marco, do you copy?"

"I'm here."

"That's the problem. You're too close. I think you're spooking our guy."

"The alternative is leaving you alone with a dangerous killer."

Maya sighed at that. Marco was acting like he had to protect her from this, when Maya had already accepted the danger. "That's the *point*, Marco. I need to be isolated, or no one will come close to me. I need you to back off."

"But—"

"It's my decision to make, Marco." Maya didn't normally pull rank, but if she needed to do it now, she would. "I can protect myself, and you'll be close enough."

"I don't like this," Marco said.

"It's our only shot. Please, Marco."

Maya saw him back off, pretending to look at a collection of Inca idols further along. It meant that Maya was truly alone for the first time this evening, vulnerable in a way that made her scared and hopeful, all at once, that the killer might come for her.

She'd only been waiting another minute or two before a figure detached itself from the party, heading toward her.

He was a young man, probably in his late twenties, with curly golden hair and beautifully elegant features partly obscured by a blond goatee. He looked like the kind of person who might have been painted by one of the artists whose work hung on the walls, rather than like one of the patrons. He was wearing a dark tuxedo and a bow tie, both of which he wore well over a muscular frame. He knocked lightly on the glass of the balcony's doors as if asking Maya's permission to come out there, but then did it without waiting for a response from her.

Maya made herself smile, even as her eyes darted around, looking for the possible flash of a knife. If this was the killer, then she had to be ready to defend herself.

"I hope you don't mind me coming out to join you like this," the man said. "You look very alone out here."

"Maybe I'm *trying* to be alone," Maya suggested.

He raised an eyebrow at that. "Are you? I'll leave if you want, but it seems a shame, when we've only just met."

He sounded like a guy trying to hit on Maya. Was it just that, or was it something more? Maya suspected the only way to know for sure was to let the conversation play out.

Maya let her smile widen, while giving him the faintest of shrugs. "Stay if you want. There are just a few too many people out there for me."

"I can understand that. I favor spots where I can be alone as well. Certainly when I get to be alone with such an interesting person."

Was that just so he could kill her more easily?

"How do you know I'm interesting?" Maya asked. "I could be the dullest person you've ever met."

"I find that hard to believe," he replied, with a short laugh. "You're wearing a lovely necklace, but you still shine brighter than it does. What's your name?"

"Maya." There was no reason not to use her real name. "And you?"

"Call me… well, does my name really matter so much right now?"

That caught Maya's interest. It *could* just be some guy trying to hit on her, looking for a one-night stand while he had a wife or a girlfriend waiting back at home. It *could* be that, but Maya's instincts were starting to tell her that something else was going on.

"If I'm honest," he said, "I've been looking for an excuse to get you alone all evening."

Now, Maya's instincts were in overdrive. This was more than just flirting. It was too much of a coincidence. This had to be their guy. It had to.

As surreptitiously as she could, Maya started to reach for the Glock hidden in her thigh holster.

She'd underestimated just how fast the man in front of her might be, though. He wasn't bothering about trying to keep his movements disguised. Instead, he brought his hands together, right hand reaching into his left sleeve.

It came out with a knife that he'd obviously been able to sneak in past the security on the doors. That knife was slender, almost needlelike, and it looked wickedly sharp. He held it leveled at Maya, a sudden edge of violence in his eyes.

"As I said before," he said, "you shine far brighter than that jewel does, so I think you don't need it to keep looking lovely this evening. Hand it over, and we don't have to have any more trouble. Don't, and you won't stay looking so lovely for very long."

CHAPTER TWENTY NINE

Maya considered her options and realized that with the knife this close to her, she didn't have very many. The old drills they'd run in training had made it clear that at close range, a knifeman could start inflicting damage well before it was possible to clear a weapon and bring it to bear.

The sensible thing was to just take off the sapphire necklace and hand it over. The problem was that if Maya did that, this man, this killer, might stab her anyway. Even if he didn't, he would turn and run, and Maya had no doubt that he had his exit from the museum perfectly planned out. He would vanish, and there would be no way for Maya to catch him before midnight.

If she didn't act now, then a woman was going to die.

"Do it now," the man in front of her snarled. "Do it, or I'll cut you."

Maya reached up, taking the sapphire necklace off slowly and carefully. She considered the distance between them, and knew in that moment what she had to do. If she'd misjudged this, she was dead, just like all the killer's other victims.

"Here," she said, and tossed the necklace to him, throwing it deliberately wide of him, so that he had to reach across to catch it.

The danger was that he wouldn't react. That he would move forward and stab Maya, and only then go to pick up the necklace. If he did that, Maya was just going to have to try to grab the knife arm and hold on, hoping she could keep him from stabbing her until she could take him down or until Marco got there.

Instead, the handsome young man's hand flashed out, reaching across himself to pluck the necklace out of the air. The movement turned him around partly, meaning that for just a second he wouldn't be able to stab Maya, and that second was all she needed.

She reached down and drew her Glock, leveling it even as he started to turn back toward her.

"FBI. Freeze."

He looked shocked, and then offered her a broad smile. "I don't believe a beautiful woman like you would simply shoot me."

“Then what about me?” Marco said, as he burst onto the balcony with his own gun drawn. “Do you believe that *I’ll* shoot you? Put the knife down, you’re under arrest for the murders of Amber Kaley, Clarissa Peavey, Harvey Jacques, and Indira Singh.”

Maya saw the shock register on the face of the knifeman. Was that shock at being caught, or was it something else? He half turned toward Marco, and Maya was there then, keeping her gun trained on him.

“Drop the knife, now.”

He did it instantly, the weapon clattering onto the floor of the balcony.

“On your knees,” Maya said. “Hands behind your head. Do it.”

He complied, and to Maya, he seemed to be moving almost numbly, as if he couldn’t quite believe what was going on.

“I’ve never killed anyone,” he protested as Maya moved behind him to lock handcuffs onto his wrists.

“Tell that to the judge,” Marco said.

“I’m not a killer, I’m a thief!” he protested. “I came here to steal the necklace. I’ll admit that, but you’re not pinning murder on me.”

“No one has to pin anything on you when we caught you red-handed,” Marco said.

Maya stepped around their prisoner, picking up the necklace and the knife. The museum would want the former, while the latter went safely into an evidence bag taken from her purse.

“You know that we’ll test this against the weapon used on the other victims,” she said. “It would be easier if you just told the truth.”

“I *am* telling the truth.”

“We’ll see,” Maya said. “I never did get your name before you started threatening me with a knife.”

“James. James Quant.”

Maya nodded to Marco. “Read him his rights, then we’ll get him downstairs. As discreetly as possible. There’s no need to ruin the museum’s party, after all.”

As Marco started to do so, Maya turned the murder weapon over and over in her hands, looking at its needlelike blade, perfect for thrusting. She found herself thinking about the wounds on the victims. Single stab wounds, the kind of thing this blade might have made.

Yet somehow, something felt wrong.

She and Marco lifted James Quant to his feet and started to walk him back through the crowd upstairs. They stayed carefully either side of him, partly to make sure that he wouldn't have a chance to run and partly because it disguised the handcuffs. Maya could do discreet when she had to.

"I didn't do this," Quant insisted, as they continued to walk him through the museum.

"You'll have a chance to explain your side of the story," Maya said.

"What side?" Marco asked. "You've done it, Maya. You've caught him. Only two days, and you caught a serial killer."

"I'm not a serial killer!" Quant said, and Maya had to bundle him through a side door into an employees' only area because that attracted far more attention than Maya suspected the museum would like.

She found Professor Allison, handing him the necklace. "Thank you, Professor. You've been very helpful."

"Does this mean there will be no more disruptions to the evening?" the professor asked.

"Not from us."

They headed to an exit, and Maya touched her earpiece. "Samit, called Detective Tanner of the Philadelphia PD. He's around here somewhere. Have him meet us at the museum's side exit."

The two of them headed for it, and Maya knew she should have felt elation in that moment. They'd caught a killer. They'd solved the case that the Moonlight Killer had set for them. Another woman would be released soon, because of her. That should have been enough in itself to make Maya feel happy, but in addition to that, being proved right would undoubtedly help her with the pressure that she'd been getting from her superiors.

Maya should have felt relief, happiness, closure. Yet instead, she found herself taking out the knife again, turning it over in her hands once more.

Something about this knife didn't seem right. Wouldn't the coroner's reports on the four deaths have made a specific mention of a wound made by such an odd blade? Was that just an oversight on their part, or even on Maya's? Maybe it *was* in the reports, but she hadn't been focusing on the specifics of blade dimensions when she'd been busy trying to understand what was going on in the head of the killer.

Which led her to the question of what was going on in the head of the man they'd just arrested. He'd wanted to talk before he struck. He'd threatened her, and tried to take the jewel. Maya frowned at that thought. That didn't feel right. That didn't feel consistent with the case as she understood it. Did that mean that she hadn't worked out the case correctly, or was something else going on here?

They reached the side entrance. There was a car waiting for them there with flashing lights on top. Tanner was in the driver's seat.

"You actually caught the guy?" the detective said as he stepped out. "*This* is the guy who killed Amber Kaley?"

"We caught him just as he was about to try to kill Agent Gray," Marco said. "It's about as conclusive as things get."

Maya didn't say anything, though, because the more she thought about this, the less convinced she was that everything *was* conclusive.

"I must say, I'm impressed, Agent Gray," Detective Tanner said. "I've been working this case for most of a year, and you found the answers in less than two days. I don't suppose you want to hang around the city and clean up a few other old cases that have been bothering me?"

"No, I think I'm good," Maya said. "I'm going to have a pretty full docket waiting for me when I get back."

How long would it be before another case from the Moonlight Killer landed in front of her? Another dangerous killer he wanted her to track down. Another foe who wouldn't hesitate to kill to get what he wanted, or who had to because of some compulsion so deep that Maya could barely fathom it.

Who wouldn't hesitate. Those words ran around and around in Maya's head as they bundled James Quant into the back of the police car. Marco went in the back with him to keep an eye on him, while Maya got the passenger seat at the front.

"So, you really played bait to lure him in?" Detective Tanner said. He sounded as if he didn't know whether to admire Maya or to be worried about the way she'd gone about all of this.

"Not something you would have done, Detective Tanner?"

"I don't think the dress would have fit me," Detective Tanner said, making a joke of it. "Plus, I don't think I could have handled the paperwork."

"You'll have to do some of it now," Marco said.

Maya could sense the self-congratulations in the squad car, and she wished she could share that feeling. She was still thinking about the killer, and about the lack of hesitation at the murder scenes.

There were no defensive wounds on any of the victims, and most of them definitely wouldn't have stopped to talk just because someone like James Quant had wanted them to. Faced with a creep trying to talk to her in the middle of her run, Amber Kaley would have *kept* running, and from what Maya had seen of James Quant tonight, she would probably have outpaced him. Harvey Jacques would have called for help. Clarissa would have tried to make it back into the club.

All of them would have tried to protect themselves.

Maya was realistic about their chances of doing that. Every one of the victims would still have died, and it was possible that maybe one, maybe two of them might have died without defensive wounds. But all of them?

Maya simply didn't believe it.

The killings had happened because the killer wanted the jewelry, but he hadn't taken it first. He hadn't *asked,* the way that James Quant had demanded the jewelry from Maya. He'd struck first, killed his victims with a single blow that they never saw coming, and then taken what he wanted from their corpses.

Quant had stood in front of her and made demands and threats. He wasn't a murderer, just a two-bit jewelry thief.

Which meant that the real killer was still in there somewhere.

Tanner started the car, ready to go. Without hesitating, Maya stepped out of the car.

"Where are you going?" Marco demanded.

"There's something I need to check," Maya said. "You go on ahead."

Marco started to answer, but the car was already pulling away. Maya headed back into the museum, the security guard not even starting to move into her path.

She stepped back into the party, and was strangely gratified to see that a few eyes still turned her way even when she wasn't wearing a vastly expensive necklace. Maya pushed that thought aside.

She had to focus on the killer. He was still in here somewhere. He had to be. Maya just hoped that the business with Quant hadn't spooked him, or she might never find him.

No. A man like that had come here for a reason. He wouldn't give up so easily. Which meant that Maya had to come up with a way to find him before he struck.

CHAPTER THIRTY

Justin moved through the gala, forcing himself to smile even as he felt uncomfortable with every step. He felt completely out of place among all of these rich folks, in spite of the effort that he'd put into making himself into something more than the scared orphan boy he'd been.

Every conversation he'd had, every artwork he'd looked at, made Justin feel like he didn't belong in that room. This was a museum full of wealthy art patrons talking about their investments, their trips abroad, the schools to which they were sending their kids. Every moment was exactly the kind of empty, conspicuous consumption that Justin hated.

He stood in the middle of the floor, watching them walking around with their drinks and their effortless elegance. Every so often, someone would come up to him, and Justin did his best to pretend to enjoy himself because he didn't want to draw attention, but it was anything but easy.

"It's all so spectacular," a young woman said, coming up to Justin. She was pretty and red-haired, with long, almost aquiline features. "To see people just wearing the exhibits like this… I never thought I'd get to see them all up close like this."

"Up close, yes," Justin said. That was a problem. There were too many pieces of jewelry here. Too many people showing off by wearing exactly the kind of thing that his grandmother would have loved. Even the ones who weren't wearing something belonging to the museum had brought items of their own to show off. Everywhere Justin looked, there were rings, bracelets, earrings, watches, all of them expensive, all of them designed simply to be seen by others.

"Are you all right?" the young woman said. She put a hand on his arm, and that was when Justin saw the diamond rings on her fingers.

"I'm fine," Justin said, although he had a hard time putting much conviction into it. He was anything but all right in that moment.

"You look as though you could do with some air," the young woman said. "Maybe we could go get some. You know… together."

In that moment, Justin realized two things: first, that he was being hit on. That wasn't completely surprising. When he'd rebuilt himself from a fat, scared kid, he'd done a good job of it. He got attention sometimes. Occasionally, he even went along with it, not that anything ever lasted.

The second thing he realized was that he could, if he wished, take this woman somewhere and kill her.

It would be so easy, and she fit so many of the criteria to be his target. It was clear that she cared more about appearances than about the reality behind them. It was clear that she put more value in jewelry than in people. It was clear that she was as bad as his grandmother, as all these people.

He could do it. He could smile and go along with her suggestion, the two of them finding somewhere private to go together, making a game of avoiding being spotted by the cameras.

The only thing that saved her was the nature of the jewelry she wore. Justin had no interest in bright white diamonds. Those didn't spark memories for him the way blue stones did. Besides, he already had a ring for his collection. He didn't need more.

He needed a necklace, and tonight was his opportunity to get one.

Not that it was easy. Justin had watched as what he assumed were two police officers take a man to a side exit. One of them was a woman who had been wearing a particularly spectacular sapphire necklace earlier, the centerpiece of the collection. It had been *so* alluring that for a moment or two he had almost changed his plans for tonight.

When he'd seen the would-be thief being led away, he'd realized just how close he'd come to making a huge mistake. It had sent a thrill of fear running through him, and for a second or two he had wanted to run, to hide, to abandon all of this.

The urge to complete his collection had overridden that desire.

"What do you think?" the young woman said.

"I think you're better off ignoring all this jewelry and going home," Justin said. "It's a room full of fake people obsessing about how much expensive stuff they can show off."

He stepped away from her, making it clear that he wasn't interested, and the young woman took the hint, going off into the crowd.

Justin let her go. His interest was in a very different young woman.

He picked her out of the crowd, watching her move around the floor in a pale dress, her hair elegantly and expensively coifed. A blue topaz pendant necklace sat on full display, attracting the attention of the people around her.

That was a problem, for the moment. Too many people around her. Too many eyes on her. Justin had no intention of giving away his freedom. He was going to do this quietly, where he couldn't be seen. One thrust, take the pendant, and walk away before anyone could see.

He'd already worked out his route out of the building. Now it was just a question of finding a moment to put his plan into motion.

Justin saw his opportunity in a moment when the young woman excused herself to go to the restroom. He hurried down after her, staying far enough back that it wouldn't be obvious, giving her time to go inside.

Justin slipped in after her, sliding a knife into his hand. It was a simple, serviceable blade, one that fit his hand almost perfectly. One that could kill easily, with a single well-placed thrust.

It would be more than enough for the job here.

The woman he was following wasn't out in the open. She was in a stall, and Justin quickly checked to make sure there was no one else in there. No one who could disturb him.

Justin could feel his fear fading away as he locked the restroom door, replaced with certainty and excitement. He knew what he needed to do now, and there was no one who could stop him.

CHAPTER THIRTY ONE

Maya made her way through the gala, trying to spot a killer. Except that had never been the plan. She'd never come here trying to pick a murderer out of the crowd, because Maya knew that was impossible. If it were possible to pick a serial killer out of the crowd just by looking, then Maya's whole job would be unnecessary.

The plan before had been to be the bait, to lure in the killer with the necklace and then to arrest him. Yet he hadn't come for Maya, hadn't shown any interest in the piece that she'd been wearing.

Had she guessed wrong? Was it possible that the killer wasn't at this gala at all, but was instead somewhere out in the city, either targeting a new victim or simply waiting at home?

No, Maya didn't believe that. The Moonlight Killer had given her a midnight deadline for a reason. The murderer had to be here somewhere.

Maya drifted through the crowds, politely declining a drink from a waiter, then sidestepping a group that opened up as she approached, as if to swallow her into its conversation. Maya couldn't afford to be pinned down in one spot right then. She needed to search, she needed to *think.*

If the killer wasn't going after the sapphire, then what was he here for? *Who* was he here for?

Maya realized then her other mistake in all of this. She'd assumed that the killer would go after whoever was wearing the sapphire, but with his other victims, he'd done his research first. He'd picked out a specific target.

Someone else was his target tonight. Someone wearing another piece of jewelry, somewhere in this room.

That didn't exactly narrow things down in a room filled with wealthy people, almost all of them wearing jewelry of some kind. Maya had to narrow it down, but what else did she have to go on, other than the likelihood that the killer wanted a necklace with a blue stone?

Maybe that was enough, though. Just the thought of it triggered a flash of memory in Maya. She'd *seen* a woman wearing a blue stone, hadn't she? Where, though?

It took another few seconds of wracking her brains before Maya could remember the answer to that: there had been a woman right at the start of the night, when Maya had been putting on the sapphire necklace. She'd gotten a silver pendant necklace that served as the setting for an Indian Blue Topaz.

Was it possible that the killer was going after her?

Maya knew she couldn't be certain. In a party like this, there might be several other people who met the killer's criteria to be a target, several others whom the killer might choose as his next victim.

Yet somehow, Maya felt that the woman with the topaz pendant was her best shot. At the very least, she needed to establish where that woman was and try to take steps to keep her safe.

Maya had only seen the young woman briefly. She remembered blonde curly hair, a lithe figure, rounded features. The young woman had been wearing a pale dress that stood out against the darkness of much of the rest of the gala.

Maya looked around for her now, trying to pin down where she was so that Maya could check around her for anyone who might be watching her too closely.

Maya couldn't see her on the ground floor, and she hurried up to the mezzanine level. There was no immediate sign of the woman there either. Maya looked down onto the main floor, in case she'd missed the woman somehow, trying to pick her out of the crowd the way she might have looked for a suspect from within an observation post on a stakeout.

Maya was searching more frantically now, more convinced by the second that the woman she'd seen had to be the target. Where was she? Maya headed back downstairs. There were more exhibits down here, and so more chance of someone being out of sight behind one of the cases or the plinths.

Maya moved around the exhibits, one by one, looking for the woman. She wasn't out on the floor. There wasn't any sign of her, no flash of a pale dress, or of a pendant necklace. No glimmer of a blue stone to draw Maya's eye.

Maya went over to a group of people, mostly young women.

"Hey," one of them said, "aren't you the one who was wearing the sapphire? What happened to it?"

Maya thought quickly. "The museum wants a couple of the pieces back for a grand finale. Have you seen the woman who was wearing the topaz pendant? I think they want to talk to her, and I can't find her."

"Outside, maybe?" one of the others there said.

The friend who'd been talking before snorted. "Like they'd just let her walk out wearing one of their pieces?"

She had a point. There was no way that the security here would just let someone wander off. Even Maya had needed to promise to be careful with the sapphire, and she was an FBI agent.

"More likely she's just gone to the restroom," one of the woman said.

"Thanks," Maya replied. "I'll check."

She hurried to do exactly that, worry rising in her, because a woman alone in a restroom sounded like exactly the kind of opportunity that a killer who valued not being seen might try to take advantage of.

Maya went around to the restrooms. Because of its scale, the museum had several. Maya put her head into one of the ladies' rooms and stepped out again as soon as she saw a trio of middle-aged women fixing their makeup. Wrong room. She moved along to the next restroom.

The outer door was locked.

Instantly, Maya knew that she'd found the right place. There was no reason for that door to be locked. Well, okay, there were maybe half a dozen reasons that Maya could think of, but if she burst in on someone having sex or doing drugs, Maya could live with that. If she left this and a woman died, Maya wasn't sure that she could.

Drawing her gun, Maya took a step back from the door to give herself a run-up. She kicked off the ludicrous heels, because those definitely wouldn't help in what she had to do next.

Lifting one foot, Maya gave the door a kick that splintered the wood around the lock. It held, but a second kick saw Maya burst through the door and into the restroom.

Maya instantly saw that she'd found the right place. There was a man in there, struggling with a woman, a knife flashing in his hands. He was broad-shouldered and blond-haired, but it was the look of fury on his face that caught Maya's eye. This wasn't a man who was just here to rob someone; this was a killer, here to murder his victim, obviously furious that his ambush hadn't let him kill and get away with it cleanly. This victim was fighting back, and doing her best to defend herself.

Maya tried to line up a shot, ready to end this, ready to save the woman this man planned to kill. The problem was that the same thing that was keeping the woman alive: her death grip on the knife arm also meant that Maya didn't have a clean shot. Even if she hit the killer center mass, bullets traveled. There was a real risk that it would pass through the man and hit the woman beyond.

Cursing, Maya reholstered her gun and charged forward.

She grabbed the knife arm, wrenching it away from the woman the killer was trying to murder, pulling him away in a circle that dragged him away from his would-be victim.

"Run!" Maya yelled to the woman. "Get help!"

Maya didn't have enough time for more than that, though, because now she and the killer were fighting.

He was strong, and more than that, he felt as if he'd trained. He used his size and strength efficiently, not obsessing over the knife the way most people would have, but rather lashing out with his free hand, catching Maya in the side of the head.

Maya ducked her head slightly, ensuring that the next punch hit the top of her skull, and she heard a small sound of pain from the killer. Maya stomped at his foot, but in bare feet, it didn't make much of a difference. Maya hadn't thought that she would find herself missing the high heels she'd been wearing.

The problem she had was that she didn't dare let go of the arm holding the knife. Maya hugged it to her, not wanting to give her foe any space in which to use the blade. She struck out with her knees and her head, trying to do enough damage to weaken his grip and let Maya wrench the blade clear.

Meanwhile, he kept hitting her, striking out with his left hand, punches slamming into Maya's ribs with awful force. He'd obviously worked out that if he could only get Maya to back up, he would have enough space to start stabbing.

Maya kicked up into his groin. It didn't do much, because her foe was too filled with rage and adrenaline to feel the pain. Another stomp did even less. Maya passed the knife arm off in front of her, wrenching her full weight down onto the arm while she kicked up with her left leg to try to trip her opponent. She didn't succeed in taking him down, but at least she had him off balance for a moment. Releasing one hand, Maya slammed her elbow down on the fingers of the knife hand. Two more blows and they opened, letting the knife fall to the floor of the restroom.

The killer took that moment to roar and charge into Maya, lifting her bodily and slamming her back into one of the restroom mirrors. Maya felt her head hit it with a crack, and now the whole room spun around her. She tried to keep fighting, tried to stand, but she found herself slumping to the floor of the restroom, looking up at the killer while he went to recover the knife with his left hand.

As he did so, Maya saw the elaborate collection of jewelry at his left wrist, all bright blue, and all very familiar. The trophies he'd taken from his victims sat there, as if he couldn't bear to be apart from them.

He stood over Maya with the knife, and she knew in that moment that he was going to stab down, to finish her. Maya was too numb to feel the fear of that for herself, but she felt the terror of what would happen to Megan if she died. Maya couldn't let that happen.

She reached up, trying to grab for the knife arm again. She only succeeded in grabbing a handful of the jewelry, wrenching it away from the killer's arm.

To Maya's shock, he scrabbled after the jewelry, diving onto his hands and knees to pick it up. It gave Maya a moment in which to pull her gun again, and now she had a clear shot if she wanted, but she didn't need it. Instead, she brought the gun up and then slammed the butt of hit down hard into the side of the killer's head. He hit the ground hard, started to rise, and Maya hit him again.

This time, he went sprawling down into unconsciousness. Honestly, Maya felt like joining him, but she knew she couldn't. Instead, she forced herself to move over to him, ignoring the sick feeling in her stomach. Her handcuffs were in the police car with Marco, but at least she could get some weight on him, kicking the knife clear and holding him there until help arrived.

Maya got out her phone, calling Marco. She knew that the Moonlight Killer would be listening.

"I've done it. I've got the killer here in custody. Do you hear me? I've caught him."

CHAPTER THIRTY TWO

Megan flinched in her cage as their captor stormed down into the bunker. He was moving quickly, and as he did so, she saw that what Tori had told her before was true: he did slightly favor his left leg, like there was some kind of old injury there that he worked around.

Under other circumstances, it might have been good to have the confirmation of what Tori had told her, but now, the sheer violence with which their captor entered the bunker made fear by far the dominant emotion inside Megan.

"Aren't you going to let us out of our cages?" one of them, Melissa, asked. Had she not seen the mood that he was in? Did she think that this was just some normal morning, where he would let them out to wander the confines of the bunker until he told them that it was time to get back in their cages again?

Whatever the reason for saying it, those words were exactly the wrong ones to say.

"Let you out? Let you out?"

He stomped over to the cage that held Melissa, grabbing her hard by the front of the gray overalls she wore. He yanked her forward so that her face slammed into the bars of it, once, then again. When he tossed her back, there was blood on her face from the impact, and she fell to the floor of the cage, staring up at him in obvious terror.

"You're lucky I don't kill you all, the way this is going," he snarled. There was no pretense of care in his voice now, no calm control. "All of this would have been easier if I'd just strangled all of you, rather than putting up with all of this."

He stomped off in the direction of the inner part of the bunker, leaving them in their cages. Megan had a horrible feeling that they might find themselves left there for a while after a display like that. Certainly, she couldn't imagine him coming out to feed them, or holding a jovially creepy court in the middle of the bunker.

"Is he just going to leave us here?" Saoirse demanded once he was gone.

"It might be better if he does," Imogen said. "At least he can't get to us in here."

She had a point. If their kidnapper was reacting with violent impulsiveness, at least the cages would slow him down, force him to think before he did anything drastic. It would give Megan time in which to remind him that he needed them alive or her sister wouldn't play his game, wouldn't do what he wanted. That might be enough to save one of them who otherwise might die from him lashing out.

"Of course he can," Lucy said. "He can unlock these cages and kill us anytime he wants. It's just a game to him. We're all going to die."

Megan ignored her, looking over to Melissa. "Are you all right? How badly did he hurt you?"

There were tears in the other woman's eyes, but Megan didn't know if that was from the pain or from the fear that she must be feeling right then.

"No, I'm not all right. He's going to kill us all. I'm starting to think that the others did the right things, trying to escape or killing themselves. It has to be better than *this*."

Megan shook her head instantly. She knew the only way they would all come through this was if they stuck together. She had to make sure that they kept their spirits up. She couldn't stand the thought of another one trying to hurt herself, and Megan had found out firsthand how futile any attempt at escape was.

"It's not better, because then you'll be dead," Megan insisted.

"He's going to kill us anyway," Lucy said. "You just can't see it."

"He wouldn't go to all this trouble just to kill us," Megan shot back. "My sister is solving his cases, and we're going to get out of here, one by one. Listen, she'll solve the current one soon. Another one of will be let go."

"Or killed," Lucy said. "You've seen how unstable he is."

"Another one of us will be *let go*," Megan replied, not willing to give the other woman that much. "And when one of us is, remember that he walks favoring his left leg."

"What?" Saoirse said with a frown.

Tori chimed in then. "It's true. I saw it."

"Yes, but what good does knowing that do anyone?"

Megan tried to explain it, because she knew it would give them hope. "The more information we can give Maya about this guy, the better the odds that she'll be able to find him, and find us. Any scrap of information we give her could be the one that makes the difference, but we don't know which of us he's going to pick for this, so we *all* need to know."

It wasn't just that, though. This was as much about giving them a shared sense of purpose as it was about getting information out to Megan's sister. If Megan could give them the hope that they might be rescued, then it would help to stave off the dark feelings that threatened to overwhelm everyone there in the bunker. It would help them to work together, and to stay strong even in the face of so many ongoing threats to their safety.

Megan just hoped that Maya hurried, though, because even she was starting to feel the strain down here, and Lucy was right: their kidnapper was dangerously unstable. She just hoped that Maya would be able to save the rest of them before things got any worse.

EPILOGUE

They drove back to the FBI headquarters the next morning, and Maya found herself brimming with excitement for most of the journey, at least when she wasn't napping. It had been a long couple of days.

Still, they'd managed to catch not just a serial killer, but also a potentially dangerous jewel thief. Although Maya was going to let Detective Dunlop have that one. It would probably make up for everything else during their time in Philadelphia.

They drove to Maya's place first, and not just because she wanted a change of clothes before she went into headquarters. The Moonlight Killer quite often liked to send his postcards to her there, so it made sense to check that there wasn't one stuck to her door or waiting in her mailbox before she went into work.

There wasn't. Nor was there one waiting when Maya went into her apartment, Marco following her in.

"What do we do now?" he asked. "Straight back to HQ to report to Harris?"

"In a while," Maya replied. "I'm going to get a shower and a change of clothes first. I want to be ready when we get a location for the woman being released."

The fact that it also kept Harris in the dark a little longer was kind of petty, but it did bring a smile to Maya's face as she got in the shower, running it as hot as she could stand, feeling some of the tension she'd felt over the last couple of days start to run away from her along with the water.

Maya was halfway through when she heard Marco call out from inside the apartment.

"Maya, get in here!"

There was an urgency in his voice that propelled Maya out of the shower, throwing a towel around herself and grabbing her gun. Clothes were nice, but in the event someone was trying to get in there, a gun would be far more use.

Marco was standing in the middle of the room with a rectangle of card in his hands. He looked over at her, his eyes lingering for a second before he clearly realized what he was doing.

"Sorry. A postcard came. I think you need to see this right away."

He handed it over. The front was blank except for a few black marks that might have been the tracks of a bunny running through the snow. Maya flipped the postcard over, wanting to see what had made Marco react like that.

When she read the message, her blood froze in her veins. She slumped down onto her couch in the towel, barely able to believe what she was looking at.

Dear Maya,

You did well to find the killer in this one so quickly. Our little jewel thief must be quite upset that he didn't complete his collection.

Alas, my own collection also stands incomplete. One of my charges decided three days ago that it was better to end her own life than to wait for you to save her. And it would *have been her next. So I have decided to count her towards your total on this one.*

Your sister remains safe. I will contact you again soon.

No matter how many times Maya read through those words, she couldn't make them mean anything else. A woman was dead, one who might have lived, who *should* have lived. A sick anger spread through Maya at that thought, the sheer frustration of it making her want to cry out with it.

"That *bastard*!" Maya snarled. "All of that, and now he's not going to let a hostage go? He's cheating at his own game!"

The worst part was that there was nothing Maya could do about it. She couldn't force the Moonlight Killer to let someone go. She couldn't appeal to some judge or umpire, because this game only had him.

She couldn't threaten to stop, or walk away, because he still had her sister. He'd been very careful to remind Maya of that, of the fact that he still held all the cards when it came to this sick game of his.

"Harris and the rest aren't going to be happy about this," Maya said. She could just imagine their reactions, now that a woman had been killed. They would see it as proof that her methods weren't working, that the whole taskforce was a mistake. They would try to go back to running a manhunt for the kidnapper, even though that had gotten far more women hurt in the past.

“I don’t know what to do, Marco,” she said.

“You just keep doing your best,” he replied. “You keep solving crimes. If this really is because a woman killed herself, then it’s a one-off.”

Assuming that part was true. There was nothing to stop the Moonlight Killer lying to her about this, and about everything else. Maybe he’d lost his temper and killed someone, then come up with this story for Maya’s benefit.

Even if she believed it, she knew that her superiors wouldn’t. They would see it as proof that they couldn’t wait any longer when it came to trying to hunt the kidnapper down.

Maya simply didn’t know what to do about that.

She sat there numbly, feeling tears streak her cheeks at the thought of a woman dead in spite of everything she’d done. She felt so powerless, so helpless, so—

Her phone rang then, and Maya almost ignored it until she saw that it was Samit. Why would the tech be calling her at home?

Maya picked up. “Samit?”

“Agent Gray. Sorry to just call, but this couldn’t wait until you came in. Do you remember the tattoo that you asked me to trace?”

Maya did. Of course she did. A snake eating an armadillo under a full moon.

“What about it?” she asked.

“Well, I’ve done some searching, and I believe that I may have found it.”

NOW AVAILABLE FOR PRE-ORDER!

<u>GIRL SIX: FORSAKEN</u>
(A Maya Gray FBI Suspense Thriller—Book 6)

12 cold cases. 12 kidnapped women. One diabolical serial killer. In this riveting suspense thriller, a brilliant FBI agent faces a deadly challenge: decipher the mystery before each one is murdered.

In the Maya Gray series (which begins with Book #1—GIRL ONE: MURDER) FBI Special Agent Maya Gray, 39, has seen it all. She's one of BAU's rising stars and the go-to agent for hard-to-crack serial cases. When she receives a handwritten postcard promising to release 12 kidnapped women if she will solve 12 cold cases, she assumes it's a hoax.

Until the note mentions that, among the captives, is her missing sister.

Maya, shaken, is forced to take it seriously. The cases she's up against are some of the most difficult the FBI has ever seen. But the terms of his game are simple: If Maya solves a case, he will release one of the girls.

And if she fails, he will end a life.

In GIRL SIX: FORSAKEN (book #6), victims of a new serial killer are found with strings, tied up to look like puppets. What is the killer hinting at?

Who will he strike next?

But time is running out, and Maya's sister's life is on the line. Can she solve the case in time? Or has she finally met her match?

A complex psychological crime thriller full of twists and turns and packed with heart-pounding suspense, the MAYA GRAY mystery series will make you fall in love with a brilliant new female protagonist and keep you turning pages late into the night. It is a perfect addition for fans of Robert Dugoni, Rachel Caine, Melinda Leigh or Mary Burton.

Books #7-#9 in the series—GIRL SEVEN: CRAVED, GIRL EIGHT: HUNTED, and GIRL NINE: GONE—are now also available.

Molly Black

Bestselling author Molly Black is author of the MAYA GRAY FBI suspense thriller series, comprising nine books (and counting); the RYLIE WOLF FBI suspense thriller series, comprising six books (and counting); of the TAYLOR SAGE FBI suspense thriller series, comprising three books (and counting); and of the KATIE WINTER FBI suspense thriller series, comprising six books (and counting).

An avid reader and lifelong fan of the mystery and thriller genres, Molly loves to hear from you, so please feel free to visit www.mollyblackauthor.com to learn more and stay in touch.

BOOKS BY MOLLY BLACK

MAYA GRAY MYSTERY SERIES
GIRL ONE: MURDER (Book #1)
GIRL TWO: TAKEN (Book #2)
GIRL THREE: TRAPPED (Book #3)
GIRL FOUR: LURED (Book #4)
GIRL FIVE: BOUND (Book #5)
GIRL SIX: FORSAKEN (Book #6)
GIRL SEVEN: CRAVED (Book #7)
GIRL EIGHT: HUNTED (Book #8)
GIRL NINE: GONE (Book #9)

RYLIE WOLF FBI SUSPENSE THRILLER
FOUND YOU (Book #1)
CAUGHT YOU (Book #2)
SEE YOU (Book #3)
WANT YOU (Book #4)
TAKE YOU (Book #5)
DARE YOU (Book #6)

TAYLOR SAGE FBI SUSPENSE THRILLER
DON'T LOOK (Book #1)
DON'T BREATHE (Book #2)
DON'T RUN (Book #3)

KATIE WINTER FBI SUSPENSE THRILLER
SAVE ME (Book #1)
REACH ME (Book #2)
HIDE ME (Book #3)
BELIEVE ME (Book #4)
HELP ME (Book #5)
FORGET ME (Book #6)

www.ingramcontent.com/pod-product-compliance
Lightning Source LLC
Chambersburg PA
CBHW030616310726
48979CB00003B/735

* 9 7 8 1 0 9 4 3 9 4 5 0 3 *